I0552329

Fallen Angel

Children of the Goddess, Volume 2

Prudence MacLeod

Published by Prudence MacLeod, 2024.

FALLEN ANGEL

First edition. January 7, 2024.

Copyright © 2024 Prudence MacLeod.

ISBN: 978-1927478455

Written by Prudence MacLeod.

Fallen Angel

by

Prudence MacLeod

Book two in the Children of the Goddess series
Copyright July 2016
Second edition

Musings of a goddess.

Kara's Tale

"It all began shortly after Penny left New York for Scotland, to rebuild the ancient altar. Kara was on patrol in the city, her powers were new to her at that time. She saved a man from muggers, then, for the first time, she met his eyes and recognized him.

"I had thought I'd removed all the emotion attached to her torture, but somehow I missed a piece of her burning hatred of the men called the *johns*. I felt a great pain as my connection to her conscious mind was severed in an instant. She killed that man with the mugger's gun, and then took his car and left the city ...

Fallen Angel

A small slender woman sat on the front porch of an old farmhouse, a faceless mask covering her features. She was gazing at the gray light that slowly rose in the east. As she waited, she listened to the sounds of the day awakening, birds twittering, small animals scurrying in the tall grass, etc. None of these brought any delight to her eyes. Those eyes remained cold, and she remained motionless, waiting.

The big pick-up truck stirred up a cloud of dust as it raced up the long dirt driveway. Icy blue eyes followed its progress as it approached, but she didn't stir. Glancing up, she saw the pale moon hanging in a cloudless sky as the truck stopped and a man got out. That cold and lifeless moon became the symbol of her new purpose.

Spotting his visitor, the man stomped up the steps and confronted her. "Who're you? What'er you doing here? This is private property, get the hell out of here."

A soft, feminine voice replied to his command with a single word. "No." She rose slowly to face him.

"What? What the hell's the matter with you, bitch. I said to get the fuck out of here before I kick your ass and throw you off my land."

"This is your land?"

"It sure as hell is."

"Then may it embrace your cold dead body and hold it forever."

His eyes opened wide as she pushed back her mask and shook out her long blond hair. Recognition seeped into his brain even as he saw the deadly nine-millimeter pistol in her hand. He started to back away from her. "Now wait ..."

"Scream for me."

"What?"

"That's what you always used to say, wasn't it? Your turn now, you scream for me this time." She spun around and lashed out with her foot. He howled as he heard the crack, and his leg broke under the blow. Whimpering in pain, he watched as she stepped past him and kicked the door in.

"Inside."

"I can't walk, you broke my leg."

"Then crawl, that's what you used to make me do. Crawl or I'll shoot you right here." He crawled through the opening, dragging his leg. "Downstairs."

"What? I can't ..."

He got no further as she grabbed him and heaved him down the stairs. He screamed again, his broken leg twisting under him as he fell. She stepped over him and went to the bookcase against the wall. A mighty shove and it crashed as it fell away to expose the hidden doorway.

She fired two shots to break the lock, then pushed the door open to reveal the torture room, chains fastened to the walls, stocks, benches with rings to fasten ropes to, small cages, whips, straps, paddles, restraints, and much more were laid out neatly. She went in then returned carrying a whip. "Inside, now."

"No, I can't ..." the whip cracked against his genitals and he screamed.

"Inside, now." Whimpering in fear he struggled towards the torture room. That voice could not have come from a human throat; he had no choice but to obey.

Once inside he turned to face her. "Please."

"Please what?"

"Please don't hurt me anymore, please ..."

"I used to ask you that," she said, a cold deadly smile on her perfect lips. "Do you remember what your answer always was? I do. It was no." The gun in her hand barked three times and he lay dead at her feet.

Stepping back to the door she turned and raised her fist, her face a mask of tightly controlled fury. Her fingers flew open and hellfire leaped from her hand to engulf the room. She let the fire rage and turned to jog up the stairs.

Once outside she turned and released the fire into the upper floor until the entire house was ablaze. Turning that deadly fire on his pick-up truck she laughed as it exploded. She walked unharmed through the inferno, swung her leg over the dirt bike she'd arrived on, and sped away. "One down and about ninety-nine more to go."

As she rode at breakneck speed through the forest trail towards the highway, a soft voice wept inside her, a voice she could no longer hear. The bike roared out onto the highway and towards a town in the distance.

THE OLD CAR CRUISED slowly through the subdivision, taking its time, but not stopping. A few people who got a close look at the driver were shocked to see a mask instead of a face. A few called the police, but the police always let her go. No one could resist that commanding voice from an unknown hell.

It was the third car she'd stolen, and it too was starting to draw attention. She was about to head downtown and ditch it when she saw what she was looking for. Kara nodded then drove away.

Dressed in a black jogging suit and running shoes she ran on, pacing herself, taking her time. It was early yet, no need to rush. Twice cars stopped, one to warn her about being out so late at night alone and without reflective gear. "Girl, it's not safe by half," said the driver.

"I'm counting on it," she snarled. He gave her a startled look and drove away.

The second one tried to grab her to pull her into the car. She jerked him through the driver's window and broke his neck, then set the car on fire. While the sirens wailed and the emergency vehicles sped to the location of the fire she ran on, holding a comfortable pace.

Night was well along when she arrived at her target. The lights were out but she could see the glow of the blacked-out room in the basement. Slipping close to rest and listen, she used her extra powerful hearing to investigate the house. As she suspected, there were three men inside, three men and three young girls. With a snarl of pure hate on her elfin features, she listened.

"I don't know, Mac, these three don't have much life in them."

"Yeah, ever since that blue bitch shut down Larry's operation, good merchandise has been hard to come by. Hell, this lot can't even speak English. They don't even understand what you tell 'em to do."

"Yeah," groused the third one. "Fuck, I'd rather die than have to learn Spanish."

"I can arrange that for you," said a soft voice outside the house. "What the hell, maybe I should at that." A dark and foreboding figure rose and went to the back door of the house.

"Mac, what was that?"

"What was what?"

"I thought I heard something. Did you remember to lock the back door?"

"Of course I locked the back door, moron. Go check it for yourself."

A naked man stepped out of the soundproof room but was hurled back inside to land heavily with broken ribs from the blow to his chest. Startled, the other two turned to see a small woman clad all in black with a mask covering her face. She leaped at them, and both were hurled against the wall where they sank to the floor, groaning.

The woman jerked the wall anchors from the wall and the three girls slid to the floor, cringing in fear. "Get out!" she commanded, as she pointed to the open door. They got the idea and scrambled away, racing up the stairs and out into the street.

The two men had regained their feet, seizing up weapons and spreading out to surround her. She chuckled her delight as she beckoned for them to come on. "Bring it, boys. Show Mamma what you've got."

One man leaped at her, swinging a wooden paddle like a baseball bat. She was instantly inside the swing, grabbing his wrist and twisting hard. He was hurled against the wall once again, and the paddle was now in her hand. Swinging it like a broadsword she attacked. Her blow broke his leg, the back swing broke the opposite arm.

The third man had a gun, and he fired several shots, but she was moving too fast for him to follow. The gun was jerked from his hand, and it was smashed into his face knocking him to the floor, his nose broken and several teeth loosened.

"Are we having fun yet, boys?"

"What the fuck are you?" asked one man.

"Me? I'm just a gal out for an evening's entertainment."

"Who the hell are you?" asked the man on the floor with the broken ribs.

"Me?" she asked, as she cast aside the gun she'd taken from them and pulled out one of her own. "You know who I am. We go way back, we do." She pushed back her hood and shook out her long golden hair, casting aside the mask.

It took a moment, but the man with the broken ribs recognized her. "You?"

"Me," she replied, as she shot the man with the broken leg. He slumped to the floor, dead. Kara stepped closer to the man on the floor. "Remember what you used to call me?"

"No,' he whimpered.

"You used to call me your screaming angel. I have a new name now."

"Oh?"

"Now I'm called the Fallen Angel. Remember what you used to tell me when you took me back to the pimp?"

"No," he whimpered as he tried to crawl further away from her.

"You used to say, 'I'll be back for you someday.'" She shot the man with the broken nose. As he slumped, she returned her attention to the man on the floor, winked at him then turned away. As she stepped through the door she turned back to him. "I'll be back for you one day," she said with a smile that didn't reach her eyes.

With that she turned away and jogged up the stairs. She took his car keys then drove away in his car. By the time the police arrived at his house she had already traded it for a stolen motorcycle.

As the ambulance came for the injured man, the Fallen Angel raced away down the highway. She was going hunting.

Payback

They say payback's a bitch, and the big policeman was soon to find out how true that was. He knew there was something out there, something evil, something hunting him. He'd only caught a few glimpses of it, a dark diminutive figure flying across the rooftops, and once watching through his bedroom window. It had no face, just cold eyes.

Kara had watched silently as the man installed heavy bars across the windows of his house. He no longer left his home unless he was in uniform, wearing body armor and fully armed.

The day after the window bars and the extra locks had been installed, he returned home to find a picture on the kitchen table. It was a picture of a black clad figure wearing a faceless mask. The picture had been taken in his secret torture room then printed off on his own printer.

How the hell had the demon gotten into the house, and how had it known about the interrogation room? He dusted the entire place for prints, but only found his own. The next day he adopted a pitbull from the local animal shelter.

Several days went by and he only glimpsed the figure twice. So disturbed by the demon that hunted him, and the failure of his security to capture even a photograph of the creature, he failed to notice the pile of bones in the backyard.

With shaking hand, he sat to the desk in his secret room and poured a generous glass of whiskey. Booting up the computer, he scrolled through the pictures of his past interrogations in that room, but they brought him no comfort. Slowly he became aware there was another presence in the room.

Turning slowly, he saw a small woman petting the dog. Agape, he watched as she turned and stepped out of the room, calling to the dog. Frozen he listened as she put the dog in the back yard. He came back to life as he heard her footsteps returning.

Kara stepped back into the interrogation room to be hit full force with the tazer. She snarled as she ripped the electrodes from her clothing. With shaking hands, he aimed the gun. "Who the fuck are you? What the hell do you want?"

"Oh no, my friend," she said, in a cold deadly voice. "I've answered my last question in this room." She blurred out of sight, and he fell unconscious to the floor. He hadn't even managed to get off a single shot.

The big man returned to consciousness with someone slapping his face hard. "So, awake again? Good, now we can begin the interrogation." Horrified, he realized he was in restraints, hand and foot. Pain lanced through his shoulders as he was hauled up by a pulley system until he could only stand on his tip toes.

He struggled wildly for a moment, but all to no avail. His struggles for relief in his shoulders changed to a struggle to turn around. His horror deepened as he saw her bent over her task. She was setting up his video equipment. Worse yet, she'd already found his full collection.

As soon as she was ready she started the camera and spoke. The voice that came from her throat didn't sound truly human. "This is a recording of the interrogation of a known pedophile. I will follow the procedures as set out by this man himself."

"No, please," he whimpered, as she picked up the flogger. The man howled in pain as the hardened leather tips struck his exposed genitals. He screamed again as she tossed aside the flogger and picked up the bamboo cane. It drew blood as the blow struck his buttocks.

"Now that the suspect is ready, we begin. What is your name? Remember, a lie or refusal will have consequences. What's your name?" He told her. He gave his address, his mother's name and bra size and those of his sister as well. He gave her his phone number and the names of special friends on the internet with whom he shared videos of his interrogations."

"How many children have you raped?"

"I don't know. Please ..."

He screamed as the cattle prod touched his genitals. "Try again," demanded that terrible voice. She zapped him again eliciting another scream.

"I don't know," he begged. "I don't. Please ..."

"Are they all recorded on this computer?"

"Yes."

She stepped back behind the camera and removed her mask, shaking out her long hair. It took a few moments, but recognition began to seep in. "Oh god, you?"

"Me," replied the voice. "Am I on this computer, too? Is there a recording of my interrogation on there too?"

Her only answer was a whimper of fear as she turned off the camera. He began to struggle wildly and beg for mercy as she picked up his police issued pistol. "Please don't. Please ..."

"I used to ask you the same thing, asshole," she replied, as she brought the gun slowly to bear. "Same answer." He screamed a protest, but his voice was lost in the sound of the gun. She emptied it into his chest then tossed it on the floor and peeled off her gloves.

Putting her mask back on, she deliberately tripped the security alarms on her way out. He was found by his fellow police officers less than a half hour later. They were horrified at the videos they found and his taped confession.

"It had to be the Fallen Angel," sighed one of the officers.

"Yeah, had to be," said another. "That means the Angel's on one of these videos here someplace. We'll have to look at them all and see if we can find a connection. Sweet baby Jesus, I don't want that assignment."

"I heard that," replied her partner. "I hope to god somebody with a stronger stomach than me gets that job."

———◉———

SEVERAL DAYS LATER Ken Jenkins finished work for the day and shut the door to his clinic behind him. He turned then leaped back, his hand over his heart. "Cripes, Kara, you scared me half to death."

"Sorry, Grandpa," she grinned. "My bad."

"Brat, you're not sorry at all," he smiled, holding out his arms for a hug. She didn't move and he slowly let his arms fall back to his sides. "You just missed Penny, she left about two hours ago."

"I know. I thought she'd never leave."

"You knew she was here?"

"Little blue convertible was a dead giveaway. She's hunting me, isn't she?"

"Kara, I ..."

"She told you why?"

"She said you murdered several men."

Kara snorted at that. "She's a fine one to talk about killing people. Her count's a lot higher than mine."

"Penny only strikes in self-defense or to defend the weak. You know that, honey."

Ken Jenkins shivered at the cold smile that curved his granddaughter's lips. "So do I, Grandpa. So do I. I just waited a few years before I moved, that's all."

"Kara, what are you doing? You know revenge isn't the way."

"Maybe not your way, or even Penny's way," she said, as she turned and reached for the door, "but it's my way. They're all going to die. Every fucking one of those bastards that hurt me and the other kids is going to die by my hand."

"Kara, why did you come here like this? You know I can't condone what you're doing. I ..."

"I don't give a shit what you'll condone or not. I spent three years crying your name, but you didn't come for me. My big hero didn't come for me, a girl with blue paint on her face came and set me free. She set all of us free. But she didn't finish the job, she left the johns alive. She didn't finish it, but I will.

"Why did I come? I have a message for Penny. She'll come back here, and when she does you can deliver it."

His voice sounded defeated, lost, as though he was already in mourning for his beloved granddaughter. "What's the message?"

"I don't want to hurt her, but I will if I have to. Tell her to stay out of my way." With that she closed the door behind her. A single tear slid down his cheek as he heard the motorcycle race away. She was gone into the night.

With a heavy heart Ken entered his living room and picked up his phone. "Penny here, was I right, Ken?"

"Yes. She was just waiting for you to leave, Penny."

"Did she say anything?"

"She said she's going to kill them all. All the johns that hurt her and the others. She says you didn't finish the job, but she will."

"Yeah, I was afraid of that. Did she say where she was going next?"

"No, she didn't. Penny, she said she doesn't want to hurt you, but she will if you try to stop her. She said not to get in her way."

Penny sighed deeply. "This isn't going to be easy."

"Can you stop her, Penny? Without hurting her?"

"I don't know, Ken. In truth, I don't know if I can stop her at all. Thanks for the head's up."

Penny dropped her phone onto the passenger's seat and started the car. "Moragah?"

"*I am here, Penny, my daughter.*"

"You heard Ken?"

"*I did, yes. What troubles you?*"

"I can't take her in a fight, can I?"

"*No. Kara is too strong. Do you want me to further enhance your abilities?*"

"No. Moragah, I don't want to hurt Kara. I don't. In truth, I'm not even sure I should try to stop her. She's not going after the victims; she's going after the predators. I know, I know, vengeance isn't our way, it's a tool of the darkness. Still..."

"*I know, Penny, my child. I, too, bear no compassion for those Kara has killed. It's the loss of her that distresses me so. She has broken her connection to me; I can no longer reach her mind.*"

"Can you stop her?"

"*Only by killing her, Penny, and that I won't do, not ever.*"

"Then it could fall to me."

"*We haven't reached that point yet, dear Penny. Kara has yet to harm an innocent. We still have a chance to reach her, to recall her from the darkness.*"

"And if we can't? If she becomes a willing tool of the dark?"

"*Penny, we must. We cannot allow that to happen. Go to the northwest now. I've created another priestess to help you. Her name is Mai. She will help you find Kara.*"

While Penny drove northward, a young couple had a midnight visitor. They were arguing and it was late. He wanted sex, but once again she'd refused him. He was now back in the living room, drinking whiskey and sulking. Still crying, she approached.

"Honey, I'm so sorry. Please come back to bed. I'll try harder, I will."

"Forget it."

"Please ..."

"I just don't get what's wrong with you. One minute you're ready to go, and then I touch you and you freeze up. What the hell's the matter with you anyway?"

She burst into tears again. "I don't know ..."

"I do," said a soft feminine voice from the shadows.

Startled, the man whipped open a drawer in the side table and produced a gun. A small woman dressed in black leaped from the shadows and attacked. The gun left the man's hand, and he was hurled against the wall. He slid to the floor fighting to get breath back into his lungs. His wife screamed.

The tiny woman grabbed him by the front of his shirt and jerked him to his feet. With the gun pointed at him, she pushed him roughly onto the sofa. "Pull a stunt like that again and I'll make her a widow. She'll never have to worry about your greasy paws groping at her again."

She turned and waved the gun at the woman. "Get over there beside him." Trembling with fear, she sat snuggling into her husband's side for protection. Suddenly enlightenment hit her, and she recognized their attacker. "Kara Jenkins, is that you?"

"Yes, it's me," said Kara, as she tossed away the gun and took off the mask. She shook out her long hair and sighed. "I'm surprised you remember me."

"Kara, I'm ..."

"Don't say it. Don't you fucking dare say you're sorry. Shit, you gave me to a slaver. You knew damn well what he'd do to me when you talked me into getting into that car with him. You had to know."

The woman swallowed hard, tears still running down her face. "I knew. Kara, I was so scared, what he did to me, what he threatened, ..."

"So you sold me out. When he was done with me he sold me to a pimp who specialized in providing young girls for torture sessions. That scum was part of a big organization. I was moved around the country for over three years until Lady Blue came along and dug me out.

"It didn't work for you, did it?" As the woman hid her face Kara snorted in derision. "I didn't think so. That's why she doesn't want to be touched. Her cousin abused her when she was twelve, probably younger. Desperate, she lured me into his car so he could have me and leave her alone, am I right?"

The look on the woman's face confirmed the truth of the statement. "It didn't work though, did it? As soon as the bastard sold me he came back for you again, didn't he? Did you get him another one? Did you?"

The woman was trembling in fear and shame. "No," she sniffed. "He wanted me to, but I wouldn't because he didn't bring you back like he promised."

"So he kept at you."

"Yes."

"I'm morbidly curious, when did it finally stop?" One look at the woman's face told her the story. "It never did, did it? That bastard is still coming back to you, isn't he?"

"He what?" shouted the husband as he leaped to his feet. "Why didn't you ever tell me any of this?"

"He said he'd kill you if I ever said anything," replied the woman, her face buried in her hands.

"I'm gonna find that fucker and put a bullet in his evil heart," snarled the husband. Finally melting under the sight of his wife's tears he sat beside her and took her gently into his arms. "Aw, girl ..."

"How very touching," sneered Kara.

"Are you going to kill us?"

"I should. Every instinct I have wants me to do just that, to pay you back for what you did." She allowed her shoulders to slump. "It's not your fault, though. I know that. Look, I have no reason to hurt you two, but I will if you fuck with me. Stay out of my way and forget you ever saw me."

The woman looked up; gratitude clear in her eyes. "Kara."

"Don't say it ..."

The woman shook her head. "Why did you come?"

"You know where that son of a bitch is. He's the one I want. I'll make sure he pays. I'll kill him, you just stay out of my way. Now, give me that address then, when I'm gone, talk to each other."

The woman wrote down the address then passed it to her. "Kara ..."

"Don't, just don't." With that she leaped through the open window and disappeared into the night. A moment later they heard a motorcycle roar to life and speed away.

A Close Encounter

Whoever knows for sure if Karma is real or not. Sometimes it seems to work, and sometimes it doesn't. In the case of Merle Downy, Karma was on his trail, and he knew it. Several members of the internet group had been murdered lately, and some had been fully exposed in the process.

Something was hunting them, and according to one survivor she called herself the Fallen Angel. Some instinct told Merle to run, and he did. First he went home to his cousin's place, but she'd talked to her husband who met him with a gun. He left in a hurry.

Kara raged through the house, but to no avail. He was gone. He'd obviously left in a hurry, but he'd packed first, and it was plain he wasn't coming back. The computer in the torture room had been destroyed and the collection of whips and restraints was gone.

Someone must have warned him. With a snarl of frustration on her elfin features she released the hellfire into the house. She'd find him, it was just a matter of time. Ah well, there were others on her hit list.

TWO MEN FACED EACH other in an empty warehouse. A girl of about twelve knelt between them, looking hopelessly at the floor. "She's the best you've seen since Lady Blue took down your operation. If you really want to get back in business you'll have to have quality merchandise and you know it."

"Yeah, but fifteen thousand? Seriously? I don't have that kind of money. The fucking lawyers bled me dry."

"So what? They got you off, didn't they? You need this one or you'll never get anywhere. Hell, I trained it myself. All you have to do is put the word out and you'll have your money back in a week. After that everything is gravy."

The men were unaware they were being overheard. A pair of fierce blue eyes watched them carefully. Enhanced hearing followed every word.

"All right, twelve thousand. If this one pans out I'll take three more if you can get them."

"Deal." The money changed hands and the girl was loaded into a darkened car. The car left and the man began to count his money. Satisfied, he put the briefcase in his car and drove away. He was unaware of the dark figure on a motorcycle following him.

He parked the car in the driveway and unlocked the house. Once inside he went straight to his torture room. "Damn, there's a lot better money in training them than any job out there. He'll be back for more. Now I just need a couple of morons to snatch me another one."

He opened the safe to put in the money. That's when his world went to hell. Something grabbed him from behind and threw him against the wall. Moaning in pain, he sank slowly towards the floor. He didn't make it. She grabbed him and hauled him to the chains by the wall.

The man tried to fight, but a fist to the solar plexus drove the air from his lungs and the fight from his mind. She threw him hard against the big wooden cross then fastened the wrist and ankle straps tightly. "What are you going to do to me?"

"Nasty things," replied the small woman in the faceless mask. "Lots of really nasty things."

He swallowed hard then spoke. His voice quavered with fear as he asked the question. "Are you the Fallen Angel?"

"Good guess."

"Please don't hurt me."

"Sorry, but you get the same answer to that one as I got when I asked you the same question."

"I had you?"

"You did," she replied, as she pushed back her hood, removed the mask, and shook out her hair. It took a few moments, but recognition began to set in. "Payback time, asshat."

He was trembling with fear and hanging on a cross. "Please don't ..." he begged as she took his own hunting knife and approached. He whimpered in fear as she slowly cut the clothes from his body as he had done to her so long ago. "Please don't kill me."

She stepped back and looked at him for a long moment, as though trying to make up her mind. "All right, here's the deal. You tell me what I want to know, and I won't kill you."

"Yes, yes, anything. What do you want to know?"

"Not so fast. I endured a lot of pain in this room, pain, humiliation, and worse. So, first we even the score a bit, then we'll talk."

His eyes widened in terror as she snapped her fingers and a flame leaped to life in her hand. She played the flame back and forth across the blade of the knife until it was glowing red.

"No, no, please no, oh god, noooooo...." His screamed protest fell on deaf ears as she slapped the red hot blade against his testicles. He fainted.

Consciousness returned and with it the searing pain. She was watching him like a child watching the animals at the zoo. "Hurts, doesn't it?" He didn't answer, he just whimpered in terror. "Well, my friend, that's what it's like to be raped. It hurts like hell, and the pain never really goes away, ever.

"Now, what else was there, oh yes. The whips, you really had a thing for using the whip. Let's see now, this red one is your favorite, right?"

"No, please ..." further begging for a mercy he would not receive was forestalled by his scream of pain, as she lashed him across the inner thigh and the burn she had inflicted.

"Remember what you used to say to me? Every time I said the word *no* I'd get another lash." She swung the whip with terrible force and once again he passed out from the pain. "Wimp. I took a lot more than that but never passed out, and I'll bet the last girl did too. That's what makes us quality merchandise, isn't it? We can take the pain." She slapped him awake.

Trembling in terror, he lost control of his bladder and bowels. "Please."

"Please what?"

"Please Mistress."

"Please Mistress what?"

"Please, Mistress, you said you wouldn't kill me if I told you what you want to know."

"That's right, I did, and you've been a very good boy, so we'll get to that part now. Tell me what I want to know, and I'll go away and never come back. Okay?"

"Yes, Mistress, please tell me what you want to know."

"Earlier today you sold a girl to a man, the same man you sold me to long ago. Tell me how to find him. Where does he live? Where does he keep the girls?"

The man hung limply on the cross, trembling in fear. "Speak up. You don't want to make me angry again, do you?"

"165 East Fourteenth Street. That's where he lives. He has a back room in an abandoned bar on Eleventh Avenue. He keeps the girls there when he has any. There's a new club across the street so people use that area for parking all the time. Nobody notices the extra cars coming and going. Please, you promised not to kill me."

"Yeah, about that." She smiled cruelly. "I lied. You've tortured and sold dozens of kids in here, so you're going to die here." She picked up the briefcase of money and walked to the door. He was crying and begging for his life when she turned to face him.

"Welcome to Hell." With that, she thrust out her hand and fire engulfed the room. He was still screaming as she reached the main floor and set it afire too. She got in his car and drove away.

Later that evening a man with a young girl in his car drove home, unaware he was being followed by a shadow. The shadow sat brooding as she listened to the girl's screams. Even a sound proof room couldn't keep out the hearing of the Fallen Angel.

Eventually the man drove the girl back to the pimp. Well satisfied, he returned home and went back to what he called his dungeon. He found another woman there waiting for him. It was late the next day before the body was discovered. He'd been shot three times. The evidence of his life of misdeeds were lying in plain sight.

Three days and three more dead johns later, the terrified pimp sat staring at the girl he had strapped down to a table. She wasn't making a sound, just staring at the floor. He tossed down another drink then poured another with a shaking hand.

"Jesus, this can't really be happening. Tell me how you're doing this." The girl didn't respond. There was no answer to give him. Nothing she could tell him would stop the pain, nothing he'd believe.

"Tell me." There was a loud slapping sound as the leather paddle connected with her bare buttocks and she grunted but didn't cry out, she wouldn't give him the pleasure. "Tell me or so help me, I'll ..."

"She can't," said a soft voice from the shadows. He spun around to see a small feminine figure clad in all black step into the light. "She can't tell you because she doesn't know."

A gun leaped to his hand. "What the fuck do you know about this?"

"Lots." The woman continued to walk towards him, showing no fear. "You see, I'm the one who's doing the killing. I watch as a john picks her up, then I follow him home. I wait until he brings her back then I kill him. That's how it's done."

Before he could respond, she moved. He was hurled back against the wall. He struggled back to his feet to see the gun now in her hand. "Unshackle her." Fearfully, he obeyed. "Bring her clothes. Not that sexy shit, play clothes."

"There aren't any." The gun touched his forehead. "There aren't any. Please..."

"Close as you can get then. Now!" He gulped and hurried to a doorway. He felt the gun press into his back and he forgot any thought of escape. He found the girl a tank top, a mini skirt, and sneakers. "Go out there, get on your knees, and dress her."

He hurried out and knelt before the bemused girl. She snatched the clothes from his hand and dressed herself. "So, what now? Are you going to kill me too?"

"Maybe, but first I think you need to feel some pain."

"Who the hell are you, anyway?"

"I'm this girl's sister," was the reply as she pushed back her hood and removed the mask. She could tell by the look on his face that he recognized her. "That's right, girl. I used to be his slave, too. Sorry I had to let those men do what they did, but it was the only way to get them all.

"So, now we come to it. Do you know where your home is?"

"Yes, it's in West Virginia."

"Do the buses run near there? If I put you on a bus with enough money for food could you get home?"

"Yeah, I think so."

"Okay, I should make this bastard drive us there then kill him, but I don't have time for that." The man suddenly lunged at Kara, but she slapped him down hard. He lay on the floor groaning.

"What's your name, my sister in pain?"

"Marcia," came the soft reply.

"Pretty name, I like it. Okay, Marcia, here's the deal. Do you want to kill this piece of shit or should I do it?"

Suddenly the girl stepped forward and kicked the man in the face. "I want to do it."

"Okay, look here, the gun works like this. You aim it with both hands then squeeze the trigger like this." The pimp screamed in pain as the bullet tore through his knee. "Now, one more time, you hold with both hands, aim and squeeze." He screamed a protest, but Kara shot his other leg.

Kara passed the gun to the girl. "Okay, you try it now. Hold with both hands. It'll jump in your hands, so hold tight." The man screamed as the gun barked and the bullet tore through his side. He grabbed at the wound and whimpered. "Again. Keep going as long as you have bullets. Take your time and aim."

The gun barked again and again as the tormented child advanced on her chief torturer. The last bullet pierced his heart, and she threw the now empty gun at him then fell into Kara's arms, sobbing her heart out.

"Okay, come on, kid. Let's get out of here." Kara led her out to the parking lot then they got into a car and drove away. Once they were across town from the scene of the crime she stopped.

"There's some clothes and a backpack in the trunk for you. We'll sleep in the car tonight, then we'll get you into clean clothes and I'll put you on a bus for home in the morning. There's some money in the backpack so you can buy food, a bus transfer, or whatever else you need to get you home."

"Thanks. And thanks for helping me."

"Sure."

"Where will you go?"

"Me? I'll go to the next town where they kept me, then I'll finish the lot of them."

"Good. I hate them all."

"Yeah, me too, kid. Me, too." The next morning Kara put the girl on a bus then abandoned the pimp's car in a bad part of town. An hour later she rode west on a motorcycle.

The Hunter is Hunted

Like a bird of prey, Lady Blue crouched on a ledge, watching a lone girl battle a gang below. She frowned as the battle raged. The girl was using just enough speed and martial arts to defeat her opponents.

A movement caught Penny's eye. A man with a gun was silently moving into position, his eyes fixed on the young female warrior. Lady Blue dropped from her perch to the street below. She tore through the gang and disarmed the man, breaking his wrist in the process.

With the addition of Lady Blue to the battle the gang broke and fled. Penny was now fending off the girl. "I didn't need your help."

"Yes you did. You were playing with them while a gunman sneaked up on you. Even we can't defeat a bullet through the back."

Angrily the girl pressed harder. "Pah, your defenses are terrible. You have no form, no focus, no discipline ..." Penny blurred out of sight and the girl followed, but Penny didn't attack her, she brought down another man with a gun.

As Penny stood over his unconscious form, a foot hovered in the air a fraction of an inch from her face. "You fool, I could have killed you."

With slumping shoulders, the tall blond turned to face the smaller girl. "You take too many chances. You play with your opponents instead of defeating them. Look at your shirt."

"What?"

"Look at your shirt."

She looked down and saw three long slashes across the abdomen of her shirt. Wide eyes returned to Penny's gaze. "Yes, I did that with a knife while you were showing me how great your martial arts are. I also found and defeated the two gunmen who would have killed you."

The girl swallowed hard then bowed slightly. "I see that you're correct. Moragah has sent you to me. She says I must learn what you have to teach, but I didn't believe you could defeat me so easily."

"I've been watching you for days, girl. As I said, you take too many chances. Did Moragah tell you why I'm here?"

"You need help to defeat a rogue priestess."

"Okay, let's start over. Hi, I'm Penny."

The girl bowed again. "I'm Mai. You have come for my help. How can I serve?"

"Relax, Mai, I'm not your instructor, I'm a fellow priestess. You're right, I do need your help with Kara, but we're not trying to defeat her or kill her. I want to talk to her, see if I can bring her back from whatever took her over."

"I see."

Mai was still a bit stiff and Penny sighed. "Mai, listen to me. If you give Kara that attitude she'll kick your ass all over the southwest, then laugh while she burns the body.

"The plan is simple. I want you with me when I talk to her. She doesn't know you, who you are, what your abilities are. I'm hoping that will give her pause long enough for me to talk sense to her."

"And if you can't?"

"I have to reach her, Mai. I have to. That girl's been through hell and back again a dozen times, but there's still a sweetheart in there, a girl I love like a sister."

"And if she won't listen?"

"We try harder."

"What if she fights us?"

"Are you always so negative?"

"Answer the question."

"We run like hell. Enough of this, Mai. We've got a long drive ahead of us."

"I'll get my pack."

Mai fetched her pack and returned to find Penny waiting in a car. She hopped in and they were soon on the highway south. They rode in silence for a long time before Mai spoke again. "Penny, I'm sorry to seem so hard-headed. I was raised in the martial arts and the training is difficult to turn off."

"Yeah, I get that."

"Is Kara truly so much greater than either of us?"

Penny sighed and relaxed a bit. "Yeah, she is. When Moragah creates a priestess She chooses the girl's attributes from the girl's own mind, her own understandings and desires.

"For example, I'm fast and strong, but my extended hearing is way better than yours or Kara's. That's because I always wanted to know what people were saying about me so I could avoid them. When Moragah enhanced me she gave that power an extra boost.

"You, on the other hand, were always badgered about lacking discipline, focus. That's why your ability to focus is so much stronger than mine. Yes, your fighting skills are way better too, but running, jumping, climbing, are my thing.

"We each have different skills, you see."

"So, what are Kara's special skills?"

"Kara was taken slave just before her thirteenth birthday and forced into prostitution; brutal, savage, prostitution. She was held in a ring that catered to people who get their kicks from torturing their victims, get aroused by the screams of the helpless, and they prefer children."

"Oh my god ..."

"Kara had just turned sixteen when I dug her out of that life. She spent over a year in therapy. It failed. Moragah made her a priestess and I trained her for many months. Kara's nineteen now and she's lost her control over whatever demon grew inside her from the torture she endured."

"Dear god, Penny, I'm so sorry. Tell me, what are her abilities."

"Kara is small, only five-foot-two, but she's as strong as either of us and every bit as fast. The two big ones to watch out for came out of her rage and desire to overcome and punish the men who hurt her.

"The first is fire. She creates and controls fire. I've never seen her use its full force, in fact I've only seen her use it as a distraction or a deterrent. Kara could burn down a building and walk through that fire unharmed.

"The second is the voice of command. That came from all the times she begged them to stop, and no one ever did. Now if she commands, people obey."

"Even us?"

"Even us, Mai. If you piss her off she could command you to hold still, then burn you alive. In the mood she's in right now, I wouldn't push her."

"So you're going to try to talk her down?"

"That's the plan. It's all I've got, Mai. I'm open to suggestion if you've got any."

Mai sighed deeply and tilted her seat back. "None you want to hear."

"You're good with weapons and potions. You think hitting her with a poisoned dart is the answer? Just kill her?"

"It is the safest and most sensible way."

"Yeah, well, my life is rarely safe and never sensible. You even think like that, and I'll put you down myself. You're supposed to be helping me here." Penny sighed then snarled. "Oh, for fuck sake."

Angrily, Penny stomped the brakes and jerked the wheel, slewing the car onto the shoulder. "Moragah, please help me here."

"I am here, Penny my daughter. How can I help?"

"Please tell me the truth, Moragah. Is our mission to kill Kara? If it is then I'm done right now. I'll walk away and ..."

Moragah sent a wave of warm loving energy through her, easing her mind. *"Be at peace, Penny, my daughter. I would never ask you to harm a sister. Kara is precious to me, too. Penny, when I enhanced Kara, I believed I had shut off all the possible feelings that could have set her on this path of vengeance. Somehow the darkness managed to hide something from me, and I missed it.*

"It brings me great pain that she no longer hears my voice. The only voice she hears now is the voice of darkness, urging her on to return the pain and suffering, to punish those who hurt her.

"Had I known how deeply this ran, I would have sent her against them myself, guiding her in the quest. In this fashion I could have held her focus on freeing other children, preventing the men form doing further harm."

"What's the difference?" asked Mai.

"The difference, Mai, my child, is that, as a priestess on the hunt, Kara could have remained somewhat dispassionate, focused on pushing back the darkness. As an avenger she is a tool of the darkness, her only thought for the pain and death she can deliver to the abusers.

"Our Kara is still in there, and it is my hope you can return her to me. If not, then run and I will create a warrior who can stop her, but I don't want to do that, as it will pull all of us closer to the darkness. This game is much bigger than you realize. We dare not let the darkness win.

"Mai, do not fight Kara. In the state she's in now, she will kill you. That is not the mission here. Your task is to help Penny talk to her, help her to remember what it's like to be a priestess, to have the love and support of the other priestesses. This is not a mission of combat; it is a mission of compassion."

"Moragah, I'm sorry I wasn't here when Kara needed me ..."

"No, Penny, there was nothing you could have done. It happened so fast even I was taken by surprise. No, this could not be prevented, but it must be undone. Find her, remind her, bring her back to me if you can, but be extremely careful."

Another wave of loving energy for them both and Moragah withdrew. Penny sighed and pulled the car back onto the road. At length Mai spoke again. "I'm sorry, Penny. I promise, no matter what, I won't fight her. She's our sister and we don't fight family."

"Thanks for that, Mai. I think we got off on the wrong foot. Your blood was up, and I started off by criticizing you. Not my best move this year. Can we start over?"

Mai grinned at her and held out her hand. "Hi, I'm Mai, your new sister."

Penny grinned ruefully and gripped the girl's hand. "I'm Penny, your bossy sister. A pleasure to make your acquaintance, Sister Mai."

———⟫◆⟪———

WHILE PENNY WAS RECRUITING Mai for the hunt, Kara was meeting some of Penny's old friends. She rolled into a small town and pulled into a garage with a dozen bikes parked out front. A big man ambled out to greet her. "Afternoon, Miss. You sure you're in the right place?"

Kara removed her helmet and hung it on the handlebars. She unzipped her jacket and shook out her long blond hair. "I think so," she replied. "Sure is a hot one today."

"It is that, girl. Personally, I'd rather see snow falling than this much heat."

"Yeah? So, why is a cold loving boy like you living in the vestibule of hell?"

"I ask myself that same question three times a day," he chuckled. "So, you think you're in the right place, do you? Not many folks come looking for the Chosen, unless they've got a death wish."

"The Chosen? You the guys Lady Blue rode with?"

"That's us. You know Blue?"

"My sister. Actually, I just came in to see if I could get my bike fixed. It's running a bit rough and over heating."

"You're Blue's sister?" With a wide grin he turned to the cooler shade of the building's interior. "Hey, Thunder, we've got family come for a visit." He turned back to Kara. "You go on inside, Little Blue. There's shade and beer in there. I'll bring your bike in and have a look for you. Name's Kyle."

"Pleasure, Kyle," she replied, as she shook the offered hand, grease and all. She stepped past him and into the slightly cooler interior of the garage. A tall man stepped towards her. "You're Thunder?"

"That's me," rumbled that impossibly deep voice. "So you're family?"

"That's Blue's little sister," said Kyle, as he pushed her bike into the shop.

Thunder nodded then spoke. "Come into the office, Little Blue. The air conditioner's actually working today."

She followed him in and shut the door behind them. The air was several degrees cooler, and she sighed with relief. "I've heard a bit about you, Little Blue," he said, shoving a chair in her general direction. "Want a beer?"

"Sure, why not?"

"Here you go," he said, as he opened a bottle and passed it to her. "Tastes like horse piss, but at least it's cold."

Kara took a sip then made a face. "I think you're being a bit generous about the taste."

"Yeah, could be at that," he grinned. "So, what can we do for you, Little Blue?"

"Do for me?"

"You came looking for the Chosen. Got a job for us?"

"Nope. I was looking for a garage 'cause the bike was giving me fits. Just got lucky."

He nodded and took another pull from his beer. "You sure that's it?"

"God's truth, Thunder, but since I'm here, there might be something."

"Go on."

"Did you guys ever follow through on Penny's challenge?"

"We did, and we still do. You got something for us?"

"Nope, I want to do this for myself. However, I am looking for one man in particular. Name's Merle Downy."

"Never heard of him, what's his claim to fame?"

His eyes flew wide as Kara produced a dancing flame in each hand. "I'm one of the ones Lady Blue rescued a few years ago. That bastard is the fucker who sold me into slavery. I plan to send him straight to hell in a bonfire." With an effort she pulled back the rage and extinguished the flame.

"Want us to ride with you, Little Sister?"

"No, Thunder, this one's personal. I tracked old Merle down, but somebody had tipped him off and his house was empty. I've been on his trail ever since. One day I'll catch up, and then there'll be a reckoning for past misdeeds."

"I'll just bet. You the one they call the Fallen Angel?"

"That would be me."

"There seems to be a number of dead pedophiles on your back trail, Little Blue."

"It's a work in progress. Do we have a problem here?"

"Oh hell no. Girl, we got no problems at all. Hang on a minute." He turned and opened the door. "Hey, any of you guys ever heard of a low life called, what was that name again?"

"Merle Downy."

"Merle Downy," he bellowed.

"Nope, why?"

"The Fallen Angel's looking for him."

"The Angel? Holy shit, Little Blue's the Angel? Wait, I'll bet that's the guy who went through here a couple of weeks ago. Looked scared shitless and was always watching the road. Said a demon from hell was after him. Wanted to know the road to LA, said he had friends there who could hide him." A bearded face appeared in the doorway. "You going after him, Blue? Want us to ride with you?"

"Nope, this one's personal."

"Fair enough," said Thunder, "but we know some people in LA. Might be we could help you track him."

"Are you sure?" He nodded. "Okay then, sure, but two things. One, when we find him don't interfere or get in the way. Two, if Penny catches up with us, you guys run for cover."

"Big Blue on your trail?"

"I'm not sure, but she might be. If she is, you guys stay back, deal?"

"Fair enough, Angel. Soon as Kyle has your bike fixed, we'll head out." He turned to the door again. "Soon as the Angel's ride is ready we'll head to LA with her. Our job is to locate Merle Downy, soon to be deceased, then stay out of the action."

"Can we beat up another pimp?" called a voice from outside.

"Sure, why not," grinned Thunder. "We'll need something fun to do." He passed Kara another beer.

Hot Days and Hard Times

Thirty motorcycles roared along the highway to Los Angeles. In the midst of the group of big tough men, and equally tough women, rode a diminutive woman dressed in black. They pulled up to a well-known biker bar with about fifty motorcycles parked outside. As they stepped through the door three huge men blocked their path. "This is our bar now. The Chosen ain't welcome here."

Kara leaped high into the air, somersaulting over Thunder's head. As she came back down, she brained the speaker with her helmet. A spin kick to the knee dropped another and her fist in the belly sent the third crashing to the floor gasping for breath.

She grabbed a pool cue and snapped it in half, then hopped up onto the bar, spinning the broken cue in her hands. "They call me the Fallen Angel," she said, as she pranced along the bar, "and I'm here to tell you, I have no fucking patience at all with your macho bullshit. Now, if you assholes want a fight then bring it, if not then sit the hell down and shut the fuck up."

"Jesus Christ, the Angel's riding with the Chosen. There's three dozen dead pedophiles on her back trail and god knows who else. Lady, we got no problems here, we don't."

"Glad to hear it," she said, as she dropped the weapons then hopped down and took a seat.

Thunder grinned and passed her a beer. "You're too cranky, Angel. Drink this, it'll put hair on your chest."

"Great, just what I've always wanted." She took a long swallow then sighed.

Thunder turned to face the room. "We're only gonna be in town for a day or two. We're not looking for territory or trouble. Having said that, we're always willing to accommodate anybody with issues." There was nothing but silence.

"All right then. We're looking to track down a piece of shit named Merle Downy. Anybody know the whereabouts of this man?" Again, no answer. "Anybody know of this man?" Still silence.

"Sorry, Angel, looks like we have to do this one the hard way."

She just nodded. "Okay, you guys play. I'll grab a bite then go to work."

"What are you going to do?" asked the bartender. He was extremely nervous.

She turned those icy eyes on him and he shrank away from her. "First I'll finish my beer, then I'll head out into the city and start questioning pimps. Sooner or later one of them will know my guy.

"Oh, bartender, don't think I didn't see you push the panic button for the cops." The man almost fell over himself trying to put distance between them.

"He called the cops?" asked Thunder. "Why the hell would he do that?"

"Don't know, but at the first mention of my name he went for the buzzer. I can hear the sirens now. Maybe I'll get lucky and old Merle will ask for protection. It'll be easier to track him down that way."

Thunder just grinned. "So, what's the plan for the cops?"

"You guys wouldn't mind causing a traffic jam at the door for a few minutes, would you?"

"Not at all. Go do your thing, girl, we got this."

Kara finished the beer then stood and leaped at the bartender. "Show me the back door or die where you stand." With shaking hand he pointed the way.

Police cars came screaming into the parking lot. With guns drawn they charged the bar, but the doorway was jammed with huge men trying to get out, or back in, or something. It took precious minutes to clear a path inside, and she was long gone out the back by then.

One policeman was angrily facing Thunder. "I thought I told you people to stay out of LA."

"And I told you we ride where and when we please," rumbled that deep voice. "You got any warrants out on me or any of the boys?"

The officer's shoulders slumped. "No."

"All right then. How about I buy you a beer and we be buddies."

"Fuck you, scumbag. Where is she?"

"She who?"

"The Fallen Angel."

"Who or what the hell is a fallen angel?"

"You know damn well who it is. She rode into the city with you."

"Yeah? What's she look like, this fallen angel of yours?"

"Five-foot-two, blue eyes, blond hair, about a hundred and ten pounds."

"Five-two and a buck ten, she must be a real badass. You brought what, fifteen men, armed and in body armor to arrest a five-two gal? The force must be hurting for men these days."

There was a round of laughter at the policeman's expense. He shot a withering look at the bartender then stomped out, his men following close behind. "All right, everybody fan out, maybe somebody saw something."

"In this neighborhood?" muttered one cop, "I truly doubt that."

"We could get lucky," said another.

"We'll be lucky if we don't find her," said yet another. "Tonight will be bad enough as it is."

"What do you mean?"

"The Chosen are in town. Last time they were here, five pimps were put in the hospital and a couple of dozen whores were at the station claiming to be freed sex slaves. Two of the pimps died, but we couldn't prove anything. No, it's the Chosen all right. Everywhere they go, pimps die."

"And now they're back here."

"Yeah, and the Fallen Angel is riding with them."

"So, why don't we take the night off. They're cleaning out the pimps after all."

"Them and a lot of innocent people."

"Innocent people, you mean the johns. We have to protect the pimps and johns? Some days I hate being a cop."

His buddy agreed with him, then they separated to begin canvassing the street. High on a rooftop, hunkered down in the shade of a vent pipe, Kara sat sweating in the heat. "LA in early August, what the hell was I thinking? With any luck Merle will have headed out into the mountains."

Her quarry wasn't as far away as that. A terrified Merle Downy sat in the small apartment, trembling in fear as he listened to his friend, the bartender, describe the Fallen Angel. Now he knew for certain who was on his trail.

Darkness fell slowly, and with it came some relief from the heat. At least there was no more direct sunlight. Kara had gotten a few spots of sunburn as she hid on the roof tops. It hurt and was making her seriously cranky. She dropped down to the street and blended into the sea of humanity.

Eventually the bartender got off shift and boarded a bus for home. He was no coward, but he wasn't a fool either. Even if he could manage to overcome the woman, there was her gang to consider. It was all bad enough to have the Fallen Angel in town, but to have the Chosen on your trail wasn't something to laugh about either.

"The Chosen. Sweet baby Jesus, a hundred or more riders, each one hand-picked by Lady Blue herself, so the story goes." He'd seen them in a brawl last year and believed it. They were tough, savage, and never backed down, ever. All the other gangs avoided conflict with them if they could. Thank god only thirty of them were here.

Nervously, he climbed the stairs to his walk up apartment, carefully checked to make sure the lock hadn't been tampered with, then let himself in. He kicked off his shoes, grabbed a beer from the fridge, then flopped onto a chair and flicked on the television.

A crash behind him caused him to leap from the chair. She was there, shaking broken window glass from her hair as a knock came on the door. "I heard a crash, everything all right in there?"

"It's all good," she called in reply. "Just a small domestic dispute." There was a laugh outside the door then footsteps walking away.

He swallowed hard but didn't try to run. "Are you going to kill me?"

"We talk first. If I like what I hear, I go away, and you have a broken window."

"And if you don't?"

"You have a broken neck. Got any more beer?" He nodded at the fridge and she helped herself. "Sit down." There was something in her voice, it didn't quite sound human, and he obeyed her instantly. She sat on the old leather couch, facing him.

She took a sip from the bottle. "Like Thunder says, this stuff tastes like horse piss, but it beats the heat for some reason. Okay, down to business. When I mentioned Merle Downy you nearly crapped your pants. That tells me you know something about this guy. Talk to me."

Watching her carefully, he took a long pull from his bottle then spoke. "Merle and I were in school together."

"Keep going."

"Merle's a sick fuck, but he was always good to me. He blew into town three days ago, said a demon from hell was tracking him. He said he could stay with some of his internet friends. He asked me to keep a look out, just in case. He offered me five hundred bucks if I could give him a heads up."

"Did you?"

The man swallowed hard. "Yes."

"Well crap, that takes the fun out of my night. Bastard's already on the run, isn't he?" The man just nodded. "Okay, if he blew town, how do you get paid?"

"Electronic transfer."

"Shit." She stood up and started pacing. He stole a quick glance at the door, but a gun appeared in her hand, and it was aimed at his head. "Don't even think about it." He sighed and relaxed back in the chair. The gun vanished.

"Okay, so you warned Merle and he ran, but he was staying in town with some of his fellow freaks. Where do I find them?"

"I don't know." She stopped pacing and turned those burning eyes on him. "I don't, I swear it. Merle phoned; I phoned back. That's all. I don't know who or where they are, if I did, I'd tell you. Sick fucks."

"Yes they are, every goddamned one of them. All right, I believe you. I'm seriously disappointed here. So, you and Merle go way back, right."

"Yeah, he kept the bullies off me in school. I owed him."

"Owed? Past tense?"

"Past tense, woman. If I get out of this alive I'm heading out, and Merle can go screw himself. A favor to a friend isn't worth your life."

She nodded. "Tell me, does Merle enjoy the heat?"

"What? How the hell would I know that? No, probably not, who the hell does?"

"Think hard now, think back. Does he like the heat, or does he prefer the shade? Does he lay in the sun to tan, or does he hide in the house with the air conditioning?"

He thought for a moment. "Shade. He'd sleep most of the day in summer then party all night. Why?"

She shook her head. "Thanks for the beer." With that she stepped out through the broken window, climbed to the roof, and vanished into the night.

Slowly the man relaxed and began to breathe easier. Trembling, he took out another beer and drained it. It would cost him most of what Merle had paid him to fix the window, but he didn't care. She'd let him live.

Ah, to hell with the window, he'd quit his job, clean out the bank account and head east, start over. He wouldn't tell a single soul where he was going either, that way Merle couldn't find him again, and she wouldn't have a reason to hunt him. He pushed the old bookcase over against the window then began to pack.

Down on the street a seriously cranky Fallen Angel slunk along the dingy street. "Don't like the heat, eh Merle? Me neither. That means you'll probably head north, or east into the mountains. Mexico's just too damn hot for us. So, where will you go? Denver? Maybe, it's a lot cooler in the mountains. Portland? Yeah, Portland with any luck. I've got business there too, lots of it.

"Okay, right now I need some salve for this goddamn sunburn, food, and gas money. Time to hunt up a drug dealer or two, maybe even a pimp just for fun."

It was all over the morning news. A biker gang had demolished a bar, put three pimps in hospital, and five known drug dealers were found dead. The police were blaming the vigilante known as the Fallen Angel for the deaths.

The next morning there were nine dead pedophiles found. More of the Angel's handiwork. The beaten men were all too afraid to press charges, so, after some negotiation, the Chosen agreed to leave town and the police were happy to see them go.

Two hours out on the highway north a lone rider dressed in black waited by the highway. As the bike gang roared past she gunned her engine and faded into the group.

They made a sparse camp be the roadside for the night. Thunder was chewing on a piece of beef jerky and staring at the small fire as she approached. "Hey, Little Blue, get your guy?"

"Nope. The bartender warned him and he lit out. I did get a number of old acquaintances though."

The big man chuckled. "Yeah, that had your style written all over it. So, he got away, that why we're headed northeast?"

"Yup. That would be why. You know, you guys don't have to ..."

"Come on, Angel, we haven't had so much fun in months," grinned one of the other riders.

"All right, if you're sure. Here." She handed Thunder a huge wad of money."

"What's that for?"

"Gas, grub, and beer. I took it off some dealers and pimps."

"So did we," grinned Thunder. "Keep your money, little sis."

"There's lots more of you than there is of me," she replied, as she peeled off some of the money then handed him the rest. "Now, anybody got any beer?"

"Heads up," said Kyle, as he tossed her a can. "You sure have developed a taste for beer."

"Yeah, well, it tastes like shit, but it keeps me in a nasty mood. I like that." This brought a round of laughter.

One of the women riders passed her a sandwich. "Put some food in with that, girl. Otherwise it'll rot your guts." Kara nodded her thanks and bit into the sandwich.

The next morning they rolled into a small town and were stopped by a single police car. The gang bunched up and Kara was lost from sight in the middle of all those huge bodies. "Problem, officer?" asked Thunder, as he brought his bike to a stop right in front of the policeman. He didn't get off the machine.

"This is a quiet town; we don't want any trouble here."

"Not looking for trouble, just a meal and some gas for the tank."

The policeman swallowed hard then squared his shoulders and pulled a paper from his pocket. "We've been informed that this woman is riding with a motorcycle gang. Is she with you?"

Thunder gazed down at the paper. It was a wanted poster with Kara's face on it. "Wanted for murder, arson, and other crimes. Kara Jenkins, aka the Fallen Angel."

"Kinda cute," grunted Thunder, "but a bit young for me. Now, my turn, you ever hear of a man named Merle Downy?"

"No," replied the officer. "What's your business with Mr. Downy."

"It's personal. Officer, let's be clear here. We just want a meal and some gas, and then we'll leave town."

His voice had dropped low and dangerous. The policeman was sweating, and it wasn't all because of the heat. "Have I got your word on that?" Thunder nodded. "All right, there's a restaurant at the gas station. What's that, about thirty or so for breakfast?"

"Sounds about right."

"I'll let them know you're coming. Right down main street here. The station is on the left just as you leave town."

Thunder nodded then signaled the riders to move out. They rolled slowly past the police car and Thunder waited while the officer made his call.

The man's eyes went wide as he saw a diminutive rider dressed in black and wearing a faceless mask under her helmet. He returned his gaze to Thunder and saw death in those hard eyes. "Everything all right, officer?"

His voice was shaky as he replied. "Yes, everything's fine. Enjoy your breakfast." He got back in his car and drove slowly away.

"Fuck it," he muttered to himself, as he watched the gas station from a distance. "I've got a wife and three kids. I don't care if she is riding with them. I'm just praying they keep their word."

They did. Thunder inquired about Merle at the restaurant and the waitress said a guy answering that description had gone through two days before. Said he was heading for Denver. Thunder thanked her and gave her a hundred dollar tip. The police officer heaved a deep sigh of relief as the motorcycles roared to life and left town heading northeast.

A Family Affair

Penny and Mai had traveled south for days, slowly getting to know one another, sharing life stories, regrets, and victories. They were heading southwest on the I70 heading towards Vegas. They had stopped at every likely town, but so far had found no sign of Kara. That morning a day old newspaper told of the action in LA and they headed southwest.

Penny was driving and Mai was gazing out the window, watching the world roll by. She'd spent much of her life in her home city, this quest was an adventure. Something caught her eye on the highway and she spoke of it. "Oh cool, a bike gang."

"Yeah? Where?" asked Penny.

"Other side of the highway, just at that intersection at Crescent Junction. Funny name for a gang though."

"Oh?"

"Yeah, the guy's jacket said The Chosen."

"What? Shit. Kara's supposed to be riding with them according to the papers." As quickly as possible Penny got the car turned around and headed back. They managed to catch the gang just outside Thompson.

Vegas had been a bust and, as Kyle put it, hotter than the hubs of hell. Kara was more than happy to spend some time higher up in the cooler air. Suddenly a car came racing up behind the gang, blaring the horn. The gang instantly spread out across the highway, blocking the road, and then slowing to a stop.

As Thunder dismounted two women leaped from the car and ran towards him. It took a minute for him to recognize Penny. "Oh, hey there, Lady Blue. We didn't know it was you. Make a hole guys, it's the boss." Bikes started moving to clear a path through.

"No, Thunder, wait," said Penny. "I need to talk to you guys."

"Oh?"

"Yeah, is Kara riding with you?"

"Maybe, why?"

"Come on, Thunder, we're buddies, remember? Don't make me rough you up."

"Yeah, well, about that. You rode with us for a day, Blue. The Angel's been riding with us for a while now. We'd like to keep it that way." Everybody was off their bikes now and forming a human wall in front of Penny and Mai.

"Whoa there, fellas, easy now," said Kara as she pushed her way through. "Take it easy now. Thunder, how about you guys go on ahead and find us a place to spend the night."

"Angel?"

"This is a family issue, Thunder. You guys go on now and I'll catch up."

"You sure about that?"

"I'm sure." He still didn't move nor take his eyes off Penny. "Go on, Thunder, I'll catch up."

"And if you don't?"

"If I'm not there by morning then I'm dead and you can go about your business."

"Not liking the sound of this, Angel. Not one damn bit."

"It's all right, big brother, you go on. I got this."

"You sure?"

"It's a family matter and nothing I can't handle. Go on now, I'll catch up."

Reluctantly, he stepped back and turned away. "Mount up." Soon the engines roared and the bikes moved out slowly. The three women watched silently until they were out of sight.

Kara sighed and turned to face the other two. "All right, Penny, I really don't want to hurt you, but I will if you make me. I won't go back with you, and I won't stop the hunt until I find and kill every sick and twisted bastard that got all excited as I screamed in pain."

"Kara ..."

"You got a new side kick. You and Tara break up?"

"No, Tara's working. So you hunted up the Chosen?"

"No," replied Kara, "I found them by accident. The bike was over heating and I pulled in to a garage for repairs. When I heard Thunder's name I introduced myself as your sister. The rest as they say, is history.

"So, Tara still doing the nine-to-five?"

"Yeah, she is. This is Mai, also Lady Blue."

"A priestess? So, two of you came after me? Still won't be enough, Penny. You know it's true. I'm stronger and I won't hold back."

"Kara, please listen to me. We're not here to hurt you. I just want to talk to you."

"I'm listening."

"Kara, it's Moragah you should listen to."

"Tried, can't hear Her. She's not there anymore, the other one is."

"The other one?"

"Another voice. It showed me the real path to power, helped me stretch my abilities and get some payback at the same time."

"Come on, Kara, think. Remember. Remember what it's like to hear Her voice. Remember what it's like to feel that warm rush of loving energy wash over you ..."

"Be silent." That commanding voice could not have come from a human throat. Penny's mouth worked, but no sound came out. Her eyes were wide and frightened. Kara had tears in her eyes as she backed away. "Do you honestly think I haven't tried, Penny. She's abandoned me like everybody else always did."

Mai stepped forward, but the voice of command stopped her. "Be still." Mai froze in place. Kara shook off the rage that threatened to consume her. Stepping close, she looked Mai over carefully. Mai was sweating with the effort to move, but she couldn't.

Kara stepped back and grinned. "This one's pretty cute, Penny. Release." As she spoke they both regained control of their bodies. Kara turned away and returned to her motorcycle. "I don't care if you follow me, and I don't give two shits if you watch, just don't get in my way." She mounted the bike and roared away.

"My god," said Mai as she released the breath she was holding. "I had no idea."

"I tried to tell you. One thing's for sure now, she's way stronger than before. Moragah?"

"*I am here, Penny.*"

"Kara said she couldn't hear you anymore. Is that true?"

"*It is. She has tried to reach me and I her, but there is a wide gulf of total darkness between us now. When I made Kara priestess I didn't fully understand the depth of her hatred for her abusers.*

"*Somehow the darkness was aware and hid that from me. It needed only for something to trigger her for an instant, and it was able to separate us. In her heart Kara yearns to return to us, to me, but the darkness has her now, and it feeds the rage and hate within her.*"

"So, what do we do now?"

"*Follow her, Penny. Talk to her at every opportunity. Sooner or later we will hit upon a trigger that will allow me to reclaim her, and when I do I will make certain this cannot happen again.*

"*Penny, be extremely careful. With the darkness feeding her abilities and her rage you could get hurt badly. Reach out to her, but be careful.*"

"I will, my goddess. I promise I will."

"*Mai, follow Penny's lead and whatever you do, do not challenge Kara.*"

"I hear and obey, my goddess."

"*Then off you go. I'll be watching closely and will help you all I can.*" With that Moragah sent them a wave of healing energy and withdrew.

"So now what?" asked Mai.

"Now we put our sorry asses back in the car and follow her. Shouldn't be hard to do, she's with thirty other riders."

They got back in the car and Penny pulled out to follow Kara. "Penny?"

"Yeah?"

"That big guy called you the boss, what did he mean by that?"

"Long ago and far away I defeated the leader of a gang of thugs called the Jawbones. I challenged them to make something good of themselves and renamed them the Chosen. We parted as friends, and they lived up to the challenge. It was just bad luck she found them."

"Bad luck?"

"Those guys are hard as stone, Mai. If they start getting in the way it'll make reaching her a hundred times harder. They're friends, Mai, I don't want to fight them."

"Well, she did tell them to stay out of it."

"This time."

"Yeah," sighed Mai, as she resumed her habit of watching the scenery roll by, "this time."

It was dark in the mountains, no moon or streetlights, just a billion stars and a few small campfires to light the world. Thunder was about to give up when he heard the growl of the engine approaching. It stopped and a small figure strode over to plop down beside him. "You took your time. Everything okay?"

"Sure hope so. I told them to follow and watch all they want, but to stay out of my way. I'm hoping they will. Got any beer?"

"Go easy on that stuff," he growled as he passed her a can.

"First one today," she replied as she popped the lid.

"Is that first one Monday, or Tuesday?"

Kara snorted and held the can away from herself. "Dammit, Thunder, you nearly made me aspirate that. Jerk. And that's first one Monday. Sunup brings a whole new day."

Chuckling, he leaned back against a log. "So, you and Big Blue okay?"

"Sure. Sisters always fight, you know that."

"Ah-huh."

"Look, Thunder, if it gets nasty and looks like we're going to have a cat spat, you guys get clear, okay?"

"You sure?"

"I'm sure, big fella." A flaming sword appeared in her hand and she used it to poke the fire then put it out. "If it gets nasty I won't hold back, and I don't want you guys within a hundred miles when I cut loose."

"You're serious."

"I am. Look, I have no idea what I can actually do, but I'm sure I could easily level a city block or more, and it scares the hell out of me. Promise me now, if Penny and I get into it, you guys run for cover."

Thunder nodded and Kyle chuckled. "Now ain't that kind of magical."

"What's that?" asked Kara.

"Somebody actually giving a shit about our survival, Angel. Never happened before," replied Kyle. She just smiled shyly and punched him on the arm. He laughed and passed her another beer.

The next morning they set out again. An old car was pacing them from behind. Kara dropped back until she was riding along beside the driver. Penny rolled down the window. "There's a town up ahead where we plan to get some breakfast. You're welcome to join us."

"Kara?"

"Look, it's like I said, I've got no desire to hurt you, either of you, and I won't as long as you don't try to get in the way. Penny, you're friends with the Chosen. I won't try to turn them against you. I've told them to stay out of this little family dispute."

"Will they listen?"

"Ask them yourself," she shouted, as she revved the engine and raced away. A few minutes later she was back with the gang, tucked in the middle of the mass of riders and invisible to prying eyes.

The gas station restaurant was overflowing with hungry bikers when the two women walked in. "You gals might want to find someplace else, if you see what I mean," said the harried waitress as she approached them.

"That's okay," smiled Penny. "I know these guys. We'll be fine." She and Mai headed for the table where Kara sat with Thunder and Kyle. "Room for two more?"

"Sure," rumbled Thunder. "You guys aren't going to start a cat fight are you?"

"Nope," replied Penny, as she pulled up a chair and sat down.

"Damn," grinned Kyle.

Penny punched him on the shoulder. "Shut up, Kyle."

"Good to see you too, Blue," he grinned.

They all made small talk and enjoyed breakfast. Mai didn't talk much, she just listened and observed. Trouble was, there was just too much going on. She suddenly realized Kara had not returned from the washroom. "Penny, Kara's gone."

"What?"

"She went to the washroom, but didn't come back."

"What? Why that sneaky little ... Where could she go? I saw her put her motorcycle in the middle of the pack. No way she could get it out of there without us knowing."

Thunder was grinning. "She took your car."

"She stole my car?" Penny leaped up to look and, sure enough, her car was gone. "Goddammit to hell, that girl is pushing her luck. She knows damn well I can't drive a motorcycle." There was a great round of laughter at that.

Fuming, Penny sat back down. Thunder was grinning at her. "So, you think this is funny, do you?"

"Oh hell yes," he chuckled, "I do indeed."

"I'm so glad I amuse your ass. Now you have to teach me to ride that damned machine."

"It's against the law to drive a motorcycle without a license."

"Thunder, old buddy, in the last month I've broken about a hundred laws, and this will be the least of them. Now let's get to it."

The whole gang had been listening, and as she stood up, they all did. "Oh, so you all want a show, do you?" Another round of chuckles at her expense. "Fine, but the first one to laugh is getting his ass kicked until he screams like a ten year old." She turned and walked out the door. Still grinning, they all followed.

Outside Thunder turned to the riders. "All right, mount up, make a hole." They got on their bikes and moved them aside so they could reach Kara's bike. Thunder took the helmet from the handlebars and passed it to her. "Can you ride a bicycle?"

Penny arched an eyebrow at him, but he was serious. "Yes."

"Okay, the principals are the same. If you go a bit faster it's easier to stay upright." She nodded. "First, this is a heavy machine, and I wouldn't put a woman on it because if it ever fell over you couldn't stand it back up. Not a problem in your case. Can you drive stick?" Again she nodded. "Hop on."

She swung her leg over the bike and he pointed out the controls. Brakes, gas, and clutch on the handlebars, gears worked with her feet. Penny worked her way through the gears several times while he held the bike up for her.

Before he'd let her start the engine, he insisted she get dressed in leathers. One of the women had spare gear that would fit her. Once she had on leather armor, they started the engine. Penny's first few attempts were jerky, but it didn't take long before she smoothed it out.

Mai, also dressed in borrowed leathers, got on behind Thunder as he said Penny wasn't ready to carry a passenger yet. They all roared out together. It was late that night when they reached the outskirts of Denver. By then Penny was enjoying herself.

They found her old car outside a biker bar, but no Kara. When they asked about it a man admitted a small blond had paid him to park it there. He'd left her at a shopping mall.

Payback's a Bitch

A large, heavily muscled man sat staring at the barrel of a gun. It was in the hand of a small woman wearing a faceless mask. His wife and child sat nearby on the couch, terrified. No one was speaking.

They had no idea how she'd gotten into the house, or when. Everything had seemed normal when he'd gotten home from work. His girls met him at the door with a kiss and hug from each then they'd turned back into the house, and she was there. She'd sat them down then stood staring at him, making no sound.

Finally he cracked under the strain. "Who are you and what do you want?"

There was a long pause before she spoke. "I'm the Fallen Angel. I want the name of a local known pedophile."

"What, so you can kill him?"

"Yes."

"Are you crazy? I won't help you with that."

"Yes I am, and yes you will, one way or the other."

"The hell I will."

"What's the child's name?"

"What? What child?"

The gun barked and the wife screamed. He started to lunge from the chair, but the gun stopped him. He looked at his daughter and saw the bullet hole in her sleeve. "That child."

"Keisha." He swallowed hard. "Her name is Keisha."

The masked figure began pacing and he tensed. "Don't even think about it. You try to jump me and I'll start shooting, first the child, then the woman, then your knees. I'll leave you in a pool of their blood and

53

find another source of information. You know what I'm capable of. Do not test me again."

She continued to pace for a moment then returned to face him. "I was about Keisha's age when the pedophiles took me, slaved me out. They're out there, always watching, waiting, looking for a chance ..."

"You think I don't know that? I'm a policeman and I spend my days on a computer looking at things that make me sick, talking to those perverted bastards, trying to set them up, find who they're after, ..."

"Chicken shit."

"What? What do you mean, chicken shit?"

"You, what you do, it's chicken shit. You know who these freaks are and where to find them, yet all you do is play their game."

"So I should just kill them like you do."

"Yes."

"I can't do that. Even if I wasn't a cop I couldn't just kill a man."

"I bet you'd think differently if Keisha was taken. Yeah, that got your attention. That made you think. Now give me a name and location."

"I can't do that. Look, if I do that my career is over."

The angel lost her patience at last. With a leap she had the young girl by the arm and dragged her off the couch. "Fine, we'll just have to do this the hard way. Since you're such a chicken shit, she's now the bait. You move, I'll kill you and your woman.

"I'll put Keisha up for sale on the internet. Shouldn't take long to get what I need with ..."

"Don't, please, ..."

"Fuck you, you had your chance." She started dragging the girl towards the door.

"Creech, Alan Creech. 117 East Tenth Street." The big man's shoulders slumped.

The Angel pushed the child into her father's arms then stepped closer. The gun disappeared into her belt as she raised the mask.

"Keisha, listen carefully to me. I got in a car with an older boy and went through hell for three years afterwords. Never trust anyone you don't know well. Learn martial arts. Make this big lug teach you to shoot. Always carry weapons, and don't be afraid to use them.

"Now, I've got nasty things to do, but with luck, what I do will keep you and your friends a lot safer."

She stepped back. "You stay here with your daddy while your momma drives me downtown." She made eye contact with the man. "I've got no reason or desire to harm your family. Don't do anything stupid to change that."

He nodded and sighed as he held his daughter close. "I won't harm your wife; I just want a ride. If either of you try anything stupid, all bets are off." She turned to the woman who silently headed for the door.

As the man watched them go he saw Angel watching him in the reflection of the mirror. He sighed again and let go of any thoughts of calling the station.

Once in the car the woman drove in silence for some time. Finally she spoke. "So you call yourself the Angel?"

"The Fallen Angel," sighed Kara. "One of the pedophiles who used me used to call me his screaming angel while he whipped me. I changed it to Fallen Angel when I killed him."

"All those men they say you killed, they were pedophiles?"

"The worst kind. I was Keisha's age when I was taken. Lady Blue dug me out years later and trained me."

"And now you want revenge."

"Damned right I do."

The woman pulled into a mall parking lot. "I sincerely hope you get it." Kara turned and arched an eyebrow at her. "Look, Angel, I have my reasons. You scared the shit out of me and threatened my family, but you didn't hurt us, and you could have. I know what you wanted and why, and I also know there was no other way for you to get it.

"I'm not mad, and I'm not scared anymore. Woman, you go do what you do, and I'll do everything in my power to convince Arlo to keep his mouth shut." She sighed deeply then went on.

"I know my husband keeps a personal journal on the computer at home. His password is Keishajean. He'll be at work tomorrow and so will I, Keisha will be in school. I'll leave the back door open."

Kara gazed at her silently. "I'm not trying to set you up; I'm trying to help."

"Why?"

"When I was that age a girl was taken from my school. I took a short cut home from school one day and found the body. She'd been tortured. You do what you do, girl, and I'll cheer you on."

Kara gazed into her eyes for a long moment then nodded. "Thanks for the lift." She got out and closed the car door.

The next day it was on the news, a known pedophile had been brutally murdered. The woman came out from work and found a single rose on the seat of her car. When she got home the back door was locked.

———◉———

THE GANG ARRIVED IN Denver to find the police waiting for them. However, they'd been taking their time on the road and plenty of people had seen them. Thunder dodged a battery of questions, laughed off a few more, then the police started to get frustrated.

"Look, scumbag, I know the Fallen Angel rides with you, now step aside." Thunder moved and the officer was suddenly nose to nose with Penny. "You don't look like a biker babe to me."

"Oh, I'm not, not yet," gushed Penny, as she cuddled up to Thunder. "I'm Thunder's new girlfriend. He's really just a big ol' softie teddy bear. I just love my cutsie bear."

Thunder was blushing furiously as Penny reached up to kiss his cheek. "You deserve that for stalling me for two days," she whispered. She giggled and gushed as she hugged his arm tightly.

"So who's this?" demanded the cop as he faced Mai.

"Oh, she's my girlfriend," said Kyle, as he scooped Mai up in one arm and set her on his shoulder.

"So, you want the rest of our family tree, or are we finished with this?" asked Thunder.

"Tell me where she is."

"Who is?"

"The Angel, dammit."

Thunder turned to the gang. "Hey, any of you guys see an Angel riding with us?" There was a great round of laughter at that. Thunder turned back to the cop. "Angels don't ride with the Chosen. Chosen don't ride with the Angels. That's just how it is. We're done here." He threw his leg over his bike and started the engine.

The police watched them ride away then got back in their cars. They were almost back at the station when it hit one of them. "Fuck."

"What?"

"Those lying bastards."

"Which lying bastards?"

"The goddamn bikers."

"What did I miss?"

"When they rode away. Those two women weren't riding behind their men, they were on their own bike."

"So?"

"That would never happen if they were claimed like they said."

The driver wheeled the car around and headed for the most likely biker bar. "Shit, one of them had to be the Angel."

"Naw, too tall, but they're not who they said they were. Those bastards know something."

The driver was still swearing as they reached the bar. The Chosen weren't there, they'd already been and gone. It took a while to track them down.

"What are we doing, Thunder?" asked Penny, as they left the third bar they'd been in.

"Just cruising the town, looking for a friendly spot to have a beer."

"You're trying to keep me moving so I won't go looking for Kara."

"Nope, that's just a side bonus," replied Thunder, as a police car screeched to a halt in front of him.

"All right, smart ass," growled the cop as he got out and faced Thunder, "I saw those two women on their own bike. Blondie wasn't riding behind you where she should be."

"Sorry boys, but I don't carry passengers. If she wants to be my woman she has to learn to ride her own hog." He grinned; Penny made a face and poked him in the ribs with her elbow.

"You know damn well where the Angel is, don't you?"

"No, I don't," replied Thunder. "Talked to her in LA. She told me to ride away and stay out of her business. Considering she's known for being tough and cranky, I took that advice to heart."

"Right, the mighty Chosen backing down from a slip of a girl."

"Look, she's doing a fine job on her own, so we backed off. We just convince pimps to find a new line of work, and we try to help a few lost souls find their way home. The Angel's methods are a bit more extreme, but they accomplish the same aim, so we leave her alone and stay out of her way."

"Oh for fuck sake," sighed the other policeman. "Come on, Jim, he hasn't a rat's ass of a clue where she is."

"What did I miss?"

"These morons are riding around town keeping the police busy following them instead of hunting her down. Let's get the hell out of here and find that mad woman." With that the police got back in their cars and left.

As they drove away Thunder turned around and went back inside. "So, we're not leaving?"

"No point now, Kyle. They figured it out. Now all we can do is wait."

"Can I beat up a pimp?"

"Go ahead, knock yourself out."

Penny sighed and slumped into a chair. "Are we just going to sit here?" asked Mai.

"I'm open to suggestions," replied Penny, taking a sip from her bottle of water.

"We could go cruise the streets; we could get lucky."

"Waste of time," replied Penny. "She beat us this time."

"I don't understand."

"There was a dead pedophile found this morning, according to the news."

"So?"

"So she would get the name and location of the pimp from that guy. Now she'll be following the johns as they pick up the girls. By morning the johns will be dead and so will the pimp. She'll work her way through the entire network in this town then move on to the next."

"So, what do we do?"

"Kara likes riding with these guys, she'll come back to them sooner or later, then we try again."

"You thought we were making progress before, but she ditched us."

"I know. Look, all we can do is try. Mai, if we get in her face it'll go down ugly, and I don't give a lot for our chances."

"She really that tough, Blue?" asked Thunder. "I saw you put Mort down, and that was no easy task."

"Kara's got different skills that make her way more dangerous, Thunder. I worked with her for months and got more impressed every day. The girl has immense power, but she's always had an iron control over it. She has a strong sense of right and wrong and that was always her guide."

"I'd say it still is," said Thunder.

"Yes and no," sighed Penny. "Look, I can honestly say I don't give a shit if she kills every pedophile in the country, I don't. It's her motivation that has me messed up."

"I don't get it, what's the difference?"

"Thunder, it's like when we first met. I didn't try to change you guys or stop you from living the way you do."

"That's right, you just gave us a challenge that made us tougher. You were right about that, Blue. We set a lot of kids free, and gained a lot of respect in the process. I still don't understand the difference."

"Under Mort, you guys terrorized a lot of people to make yourselves feel tough. As the Chosen you terrorized a lot of really bad people, helped a lot of innocents, and became stronger. You now feel better about yourselves than before. Now you help people just because you can, and it feels good. Deny it if you can."

"Naw, you're right about that. So, back to Little Blue, what's the difference there?"

"Right now something's gone wrong inside her. She's out for revenge and that leads down a dark path. If she was doing it to help the victims, I'd help her. I'm not here to try to stop her, Thunder. I just want to help her get her head straight again."

"I still think there's something going on you're not telling."

"Sure you want to know?"

"Not really," he grunted. "I get the impression it'd all be over my head anyway." She gazed at him for a moment then he sighed. "Okay, just sketch it out for me."

She smiled and patted his arm. "There's a cosmic battle going on between the dark and the light."

"Good versus evil?"

"Something like that."

"I'd have to say evil's winning."

"And then some."

"So, you guys are the warriors for the good, and Angel's slipped over to the darkside?"

"Something like that, but not quite. We can still get her back. I know we can still get her back."

"Okay, so where do we fit in?"

"Just keep doing what you're doing, Thunder. Help her, but don't get between us if it gets ugly."

"Gotcha. So, what's your next move, if you don't mind my asking."

"We've lost this one. We have to figure out where she'll go next and get there ahead of her. Got any ideas you'd care to share?"

"Sure, just locate old Merle."

"Who the heck is Merle?"

"Merle Downy, he's the guy who sold her into slavery in the first place. Angel's tracking him and he's on the run. He's a nasty piece of work, and he stays with the pedophiles in whatever town he lands in. Where he goes is where she'll go next.

"Merle apparently doesn't like the heat, so he left LA. We tracked him to Vegas and then on to Denver. Cooler up in the mountains, see."

"You're being awfully helpful, Thunder. What are you up to?"

"Angel told me to, Blue. She said she just wants you to stay out of it. She knows you're following her, and she just wants us to slow you down a bit."

"So she can get to Merle first."

"Oh yeah. Man's already dead, just doesn't have enough sense to lay down."

"There's more to this," said Mai.

"Isn't it obvious?" sighed Penny.

"Kara is a tool of the darkness now. By keeping us busy, she keeps us away from fighting the dark in other places, right?"

"Yeah, I'd say that's it."

"Is there more, Penny?"

"Yeah, there is. I expect the dark will eventually try to cause a fight between us and Kara. With you and I dead, it'll be a big setback to the light. Mai, no matter what, you must never try to fight her."

Mai nodded then relaxed into her chair. "So, what do we do? If it comes to that, I mean."

"We run like hell and hope we make it," replied Penny, her shoulders slumping.

———— ◉ ————

ACROSS TOWN A MAN SAT trembling in fear. He'd been stripped naked and bound hand and foot. She'd left him there on the floor while she'd cut down the child he had chained to the wall. He whimpered as she hooked him to the pulley and hauled him up until he was hanging from the wrists.

"Take this," she said as she passed a whip to the child. "Here's what we'll do, you and me. I want answers, and this man has them. I'll ask him a question, and if he lies to me or doesn't answer, you use the whip on him until he screams, okay?"

A snarl of pure hate crossed the child's face as she nodded and turned towards the hapless man. "Go ahead, take a few practice swings to get the feel of it."

With a look of glee the child swung the whip. It smacked against his bare back and he yelped. "Think now," she said to the girl. "Where does he like to hit you?" The child swung the whip again with more gusto. The man screamed as it struck the back of his bare legs.

Suddenly the child went crazy, flailing away at her helpless tormentor. He screamed and screamed, but Kara let the child go until her arms grew too tired to swing the whip. She patted the girl's shoulder. "Okay now, he's got the idea. You rest while I ask a few questions."

She turned to the whimpering man. "Do you know who I am?"

"No."

She pushed the mask up over her head and shook out her long blond hair. "How about now? Take your time. Do you know who I am?" Recognition slowly crept into his eyes. "Well?"

"Yes," he whimpered.

"You used to call me slave, but I have a new name now. Now I'm the Fallen Angel. Tell me, what was your favorite toy to use on me."

He just whimpered, but didn't answer. The child swung the whip with gusto against the back of his legs. "The paddle," he screamed as she struck again, "the paddle."

"That's right," replied Kara, "the paddle." She picked up the long handled leather paddle and smiled wickedly. "Now for the big question. Do you know a man named Merle Downy?"

"Oops, too slow," she said as she passed the weapon to the child.

"No, wait, I ..." he screamed as the girl struck him on the genitals with the leather. "Yes, yes," he sobbed as he hung limply in the chains.

"Now we're getting somewhere. You know Merle. Where is he?"

"I don't know ..." She nodded to the child and the leather made a loud smack as it struck. "Salt Lake City, Salt Lake City, please ..."

"Okay, great, that's what I wanted to know. Now, what should we do with this piece of misery?"

For the first time the child spoke. It was only two words and it was so soft Kara could barely hear her. "Kill him."

The Angel nodded and the man started to weep and beg. She whipped out a gun and shot him through the heart. "Come on kid, let's get out of this rotten place."

"We should set it on fire so nobody else will be able to use it."

Kara turned and looked at the girl. "You really want to?" She nodded. "Okay, you got it." She thrust out her hand and an inferno of flame leaped to life in the house they had just left. She let her arm fall back and put the child in the car. They soon passed the fire engine going the other way.

On the Road Again

"Hey kid, you can't go in there," said the beefy man at the door. The girl ducked past him and ran in to the bar calling out, "Thunder, Thunder ..." the doorman caught her by the collar but a tall man stood in his way.

"Hold on a minute," said that impossibly deep voice.

"This is a bar. The kid can't be in here."

"I know. Just give me a second, I'll get her out of here." The man nodded then returned to his post. "Okay, kid, I'm Thunder. You got a message for me?"

"Angel said I could ride with you, she said you'd keep me safe."

"Don't you want to go home?"

"Mom's in jail, got no father, and I was in foster care until my foster father sold me."

"Life on the road better than what you had?" She nodded. "Can you read and write?"

"Yeah, sure."

"Then you'll study as the occasion arises, agreed?"

She nodded. He blew a loud whistle then walked out of the bar, the girl right beside him. The rest of the gang soon joined them in the parking lot. "What's your name, kid?"

"She gave me a new one. She said I could be called Ryder because you'll teach me to ride."

"Did she now? Okay, but for now you ride behind me. People, this is Ryder. She'll be keeping us company for a few years."

There were a few grunts of acknowledgment, but it was Penny who objected. "Thunder, I'm not sure this is wise."

"Angel sent her to us, Blue. You can guess where she found her. Ryder says she has no family and was snatched from foster care, doesn't want to go back. She'll ride with me; I'll take care of her."

"Blue, are you Lady Blue?"

"Yes, I've been called that."

"She said to tell you she's on her way to Salt Lake City."

Penny sighed and relented. "Did she kill the guy?"

"Yeah, but she let me whip the bastard first. She set the place on fire when we left."

"Ryder, the Chosen lead a rough life, but it'll be better than what you had, I guess. They'll protect you, but you'll have to be totally loyal to them, too. That's how it works. Can you do that?"

"Yeah, I think so. Angel said I could pretend Thunder was my dad until I get old enough."

"How old are you?"

"Sixteen." Penny arched an eyebrow at her. "Fifteen."

"All right, Ryder. Thunder, Mai, and I are headed for Salt Lake City."

"Us too, Blue."

"You know what she's doing, don't you?" said Mai.

"Sure. Ryder's about her size. If the cops stop us they'll think Ryder is her until the helmet comes off and they realize she's just a kid."

"So, what's the plan?"

"We ride out, find someplace outside the city to camp for the night."

"Camping? We're going camping?"

"Yeah, kid," grinned Thunder. "You up for it?"

"Hell yeah, never been camping before. Oh, Blue, here's your car keys. She said to give them back."

"Ah, dammit, she took the bike back."

"Starting to enjoy a real ride, eh Blue?"

"Yeah, Thunder, I was. Lead me to a place I can get a fast bike. You'll need leathers and a helmet for Ryder anyway. She can ride in the car with us until we get her outfitted." He nodded and turned to his bike.

Penny sold the car on the old lot next to the bike shop then paid cash for the bike. They also got new leathers for her, Mai, and Ryder. Once everybody was ready they set out and left the city. Darkness had fallen before they stopped at a campsite and settled in for the night.

Far out ahead of them a lone rider sped on through the moonlight. Like a hunting hound on a fresh scent, the Fallen Angel perused her prey. "You can run, but I'll find you, you miserable bastard. You'll pay for what you did to me, and you'll pay for what the rest of them did to me. You're a dead man, Merle Downy, but you'll go out slow."

Even as she approached Salt Lake City, a man in an old car left town, headed for Seattle, maybe even Canada. He had contacts in both places. Finally he decided on Seattle, no issues at the border. He sighed with relief as he read the text message on his phone. Her bike gang had just left Denver, a small rider with them. Merle eased back on the gas; he had a good lead.

Kara had a name in Salt Lake City. She'd never been there, so she had no real axe to grind, but what the hell. A quick look through a phone book turned up an address.

There was nobody home, so she broke the lock on the back door and slipped inside. It didn't take her long to find the hidden room. She returned to the living room and spent the rest of the day trying to guess the password to his computer. Eventually she gave that up and grabbed a nap.

The sound of a key in the front door alerted her to his return. The man went straight to his computer and fired it up, a smile on his face. Yes, there were new messages with pics.

Grabbing the laptop he hurried down to the dungeon. He was barely three steps inside when he realized something was wrong. Too late, the door clicked shut behind him.

Wide eyed, he stood frozen, staring at the small figure dressed in black and wearing a faceless mask. "Put it down," she said, her voice cold as a winter's wind. He carefully placed the laptop on the floor. "Step away from it." Silently, he obeyed.

"Good boy."

"Are you going to kill me?"

"Maybe. Depends. Where is Merle Downy?"

"I don't know."

A gun leaped to her hand. "Try again."

"I don't know, Seattle or Vancouver, Canada," he stammered. "He hadn't decided when he left. Please don't kill me ..."

"Shut the hell up. Do you know who Merle's contacts in Seattle are?"

"They'd be on the contact list, but there's no way to know who they really are unless ..."

"Unless you'd already met them. Step over here to the desk. Write down the names and addresses of the ones you know in Seattle." With shaking hand, he complied. "Okay, now we're cooking. Since you and I've never met, I've no real reason to kill you. So, you phone the cops, confess your sins, and I'll let you live."

He just stared at her with his mouth hanging open. She slipped the safety off the gun and smiled coldly. Weeping, he made the call. When he was done she herded him upstairs. A sharp crack on the jaw and he fell unconscious to the floor. She kicked open the front door and left. She was long gone when the police arrived.

The Chosen were gaining on a single rider as a police car approached from the next town. The lights came up just as the gang engulfed the lone biker. They all stopped and the officer got out to approach. "Morning, Officer," rumbled that deep voice. "Something wrong?"

"Maybe, maybe not. I just have a few questions for you."

"All right. Ask away."

"Where you headed?"

"Depends, actually. I'm thinking Seattle, though."

"You're the Chosen, am I right?"

"Right as rain."

"This is a quiet little town; we don't want any trouble here."

"Most are and none do," replied Thunder. "We're not looking to cause trouble, just get some gas and grub then we'll be on our way."

"Works for me. Just one more thing," said the officer. "Point out the Angel and the rest of you can go about your business."

"That again," said Thunder. "I've explained this to you cops before, the Angels don't ride with the Chosen. Chosen don't ride with the Angels. That's just how it is."

"That's not what I meant, and you damn well know it. I want the murderer known as the Fallen Angel. She rides with you. Point her out and I'll let you go."

Thunder suddenly became aware of the child's hands around his waist trembling. He sighed deeply and patted those hands. "Ryder, you go back and get on with Marla now." The youngster hopped off and ran to another motorcycle. She climbed up behind the woman as Thunder dismounted from his bike.

The policeman backed away and drew his gun as Thunder faced him, hooking his thumbs into his belt. "So, you planning to shoot me now and write up some bullshit story about me resisting arrest?" The cop swallowed hard.

"Yeah, well let me explain something to you," Thunder went on. "First, you pull that trigger and you won't live long enough to make that report. Second, when the Chosen are done with you, they'll rip the guts out of your tiny town then burn it to the ground. Let that sink in for a minute.

"All right, now that you have an idea of what's at stake here, you have a decision to make. Are you going to leave us in peace to have breakfast then hit the road again, or are you willing to be responsible for what happens next?"

The man's hands were shaking and he was keenly aware that there were at least a dozen guns trained on him. He backed away and put his gun back in the holster. Silently he watched as the riders moved out towards town.

The officer nearly wet himself as a diminutive woman wearing a faceless mask rode slowly by. She hadn't gone far when she turned around and came back, sitting silently on the bike, staring at him. After a few minutes she sped away, returning to her place in the middle of the group.

The officer was shaking with fear as he got back in his car. He radioed in that he wasn't feeling well and was going home for the day. Terror gripped his heart as he packed to flee. He knew who was wearing that mask, and he knew she recognized him for what he was.

As they sat around the table enjoying breakfast, Thunder broached the question. "So, you know that cop, little sis?"

"Oh yeah, I remember him all right. He spent a week in Portland a couple of years ago. We had a whole week together."

"Kara ..."

"Don't say it, Penny. Don't even think it." She took her plate and went to join Kyle, Marla, and Ryder.

"So, Ryder, how're you making out? Everything okay?"

"Yeah." The girl didn't raise her eyes from the plate.

"You recognized the cop too, didn't you?"

"Yeah."

"The cop?" asked Penny as she joined them. "You too?" She was looking right at the girl.

"Yeah, me too. Angel, are you going to kill him?"

"No she's not."

"Penny, I warned you ..."

"No, Kara, let me deal with this. I swear to you he'll never get his hands on a child again."

"But he'll live."

"For a while, anyway, if he behaves himself."

"Why, Penny?"

"Look, Kara, I've told you before, I have no problem with those scum meeting their fate. I don't."

"But?"

"I want you back, my sister. I want you back in Moragah's arms with me. Come back, Kara, and I'll help you clean them out. We'll take them all down together so they'll never hurt another child ever again. Come on back, you know you want to."

Kara actually wavered, Penny saw it in her eyes, but she didn't have time. Five police officers charged into the restaurant with guns drawn. "Nobody move a muscle. Hands in the air where we can see them, now. Everybody ..."

"Whoa, officer, whoa," grinned Kara, as she stood up with her hands over her head. "Easy now. You're looking for me, right? I'm the one you want. These guys are just a bunch of easy riders I met on the road. Here's the deal, you take me and let these folks go about their business."

"We don't make deals with murderers. Get on the floor now, face down now." She complied and her arms were roughly jerked behind her back and heavy restraints clamped on her. As they hauled her to her feet she winked at Thunder. Penny saw it and swallowed hard.

"The rest of you stay right where you are. The meat wagon will be here for you in a minute," snarled the policeman as two others dragged Kara away.

"This is a mistake, officer," Penny said as she approached him slowly. "Sir, think about what you're doing, think about the people of this town. What do you think is going to happen here once the rest of their gang hears about this?"

"So tell me, what do you think will happen?"

"One day soon the rest of them will arrive with every other gang that owes affiliation or a favor. You'll be facing nearly a thousand motorcycles on the streets, your town will become a war zone. Officer, you have who you wanted. You've caught the Fallen Angel. You've got your murderer."

"Yes and the rest of you are accessories to her crimes."

"That's going to be damned hard to prove, and the media will have a field day with it. They already want to pin a medal on the Angel. Think about this. Think about what will happen to the town. To serve and protect, right? How is this going to serve or protect?"

"So I should just let these people go to protect the town?" he sneered.

"That's what I'm saying."

"Not going to happen." He was startled at how fast she moved.

In a heartbeat all three officers were down and groaning. She dropped their guns on the floor beside them. "Look at me, moron. I'm a girl half your size, and I just put three of you down. What the hell do you think will happen if these guys get involved?" She hauled him to his feet.

The manager of the restaurant stepped in. "Jim, she's right. Think about this. Jesus, if they go wild on the town there'll be nothing left. You got your prisoner. Let these folks go."

Suddenly the cop grabbed Penny and shoved her against the counter. "You're under arrest for assaulting a police officer. The rest of you have ten minutes to get out of town." Mai turned away to stifle a grin as Penny winked at her.

With guns still in their hands, the police backed out of the building, stuffed Penny into the back of their car, then drove away. "Breakfast is on the house," said the manager as Thunder approached to pay the bill for the gang.

"Can't make a living that way, brother," replied Thunder. He paid the bill and added a generous tip. "Listen, if all this turns ugly, I'll make sure this establishment is off limits. You hear too many motors on the street, you get your family down here pronto."

The man had relief written all over his face. "Thank you."

"Now, we'll be leaving one bike, maybe two here ..."

"One," said Mai.

"One bike for a while," grinned Thunder. "Somebody will pick it up later today or early tomorrow, that all right with you?"

"Yes, of course."

"Obliged."

The gang rode away and the town gave a sigh of relief. Once out of town Mai pulled over and waited while the others went on ahead.

Meanwhile, at the police station, both Penny and Kara had been processed, then put in adjoining cells. Kara was pacing around, inspecting every detail of the holding area. Penny winked at her as she was brought in.

The big cop sneered at Kara. "Forget it, Angel. There's no way in hell you could bust out of here. Besides, these cells are under constant surveillance."

"Oh yeah? I've heard these things have a habit of overheating." Penny snickered at that.

"Your gang rode away and left you," gloated the cop.

"Not my gang," replied Kara, as she continued her inspection. Suddenly there was a sizzling sound and smoke began to pour from the ceiling where the hidden camera was placed. "Whoops, told ya. About the gang, you were smart to let them go."

"Oh you think so?"

"Yeah, I do. Thing is, you've got nothing on them anyway, I met them on the road, they figured out who I am and said I could ride along since we were going the same way, but they won't defend me. I haven't earned my colors yet."

"Really, so what do you have to do to earn Chosen colors?"

"You don't want to know. Go away now, I'm tired of talking to you." He started to bluster, but she cut him off. "Go!" He turned on his heel and marched to the outer office.

Kara turned to Penny. "Now or later?"

"After dark."

"The bastard'll be long gone by then. We're wasting time."

"Kara, leave that guy to me, all right?"

"No, Penny. It'll be too dangerous for you to stay in town."

"Then let's do this together."

Kara flopped down on the bunk and grabbed her head. The pain was intense, but she fought it. Penny was shocked to hear her fighting with the voice of the dark. Kara snarled and jumped up again. "No, fuck you and the horse you rode in on. I have no quarrel with Penny, I won't fight her unless she gives me no other choice.

"No, I won't, and even you can't make me do anything I don't want to. I'm in control now. Shut the hell up and get the fuck out of my head. Penny, you swear to bring that bastard down?"

"I do, my sister. I promise I will."

"Then let's get to work. She turned and shot a gout of fire into the passageway between the cells. The sprinklers came on, but they couldn't handle the intensity of the heat. Kara created a spike of intense fire and melted the lock on her cell door as the policemen rushed in.

They opened Penny's cell then turned to Kara, but she was already out and on the attack. Penny knocked out the last two and helped Kara drag them outside.

Once they were clear the Fallen Angel turned and sent raging hellfire into the police station. It fairly exploded in flames. To the horror of the police, she turned and ran back inside as the fire consumed the building and drove them back. It took some time before they noticed someone had stolen a cruiser and driven off. Lady Blue was gone.

The police sergeant sat on the grass watching the fire department fight the inferno the station had become. For a moment they'd had it all. They'd caught Penny Preston, aka Lady Blue, plus they'd captured the Fallen Angel.

They'd had them both. Now they were both gone, the Angel dead in the fire, no one could have survived that, and Lady Blue gone in a stolen police cruiser.

Across town, a man hurriedly stuffed the last of the incriminating evidence into the back of his car. He'd already erased everything from his computer. He hurried to the car with the last of it as a cruiser blasted into the driveway, blocking his escape.

A woman dressed in black with a blue spiral on her forehead grabbed him and hurled him back against the side of the house. "What the fuck? Who the hell are you?"

"I'm Lady Blue, and you're a low life scumbag of a pedophile. You have once chance to live. Call your fellow officers and confess everything."

"And if I don't?"

"You die." He whipped out his gun, but she was already moving. She battered aside the gun then shattered his jaw with a kick. Her next blow ended his life. Penny came down off combat mode and spat on the body. "Warned you." She turned and shifted back onto combat mode.

She reached the restaurant to find Mai waiting on the bike. Kara was gone. Penny hopped on behind Mai and the bike sped away; they caught up with the gang at sundown. They were just setting up camp.

"Is it done, Penny?" asked Kara.

"It's done," sighed Penny. "He's dead."

Kara nodded. "Okay, this has been fun and all, guys, but it's all falling to shit."

"You think?" grinned Kyle as he tossed her a beer.

"Yeah, I think. Look, they're convinced I'm riding with you guys and next time they'll come at you heavy. Go home, guys. You've got Ryder to look out for now. Go home.

"They'll look for me with you for a while, but if I'm not there they'll have no reason to give you a hard time. Meanwhile, I'll be on the road alone and they'll ignore me cause they'll be looking for a gang."

"It does make a crazy kind of sense," agreed Thunder. "I gotta tell you, Angel. No matter how much sense it makes, I don't like it and I don't want it. You're one of the Chosen now. We don't abandon our own, no matter what." There was a general round of agreement from the others.

"Okay, tell you what," sighed Kara. "I'll finish up what I've got to do, then I'll join you back at the garage. Sorry big brother, it's the best I've got. Right now I'm putting you all in too much danger." That brought a round of laughter from the group.

"You guys are all nuts," she sighed as she stood up. "Go home. I'll meet you there in a few months." With that, she strode to her bike and jumped on, Penny and Mai swiftly following behind, but there was no need. A moment later they all laughed again at the sound of Kara's voice.

"Kyle, you fucker, why won't my bike start?"

"I don't know," he replied, laughter clear in his voice. "Maybe it needs a spark plug." Another round of laughter.

"Kyle you bone head, give me back my spark plug."

"Not until you stop trying to leave us. Come on back and have another beer, it'll clear your mind, help you make sense."

"Thunder, make him give me back my spark plug."

"Sorry, sis, I can't do a damn thing with him, never could."

"Come on, guys ..."

"The Chosen don't abandon their own, little sis," replied Thunder. "That includes you. Come on back and have another beer. We'll all head out in the morning."

"Yeah, and what happens if there's a hundred cops waiting for us?"

"There won't be."

"What makes you so sure?"

"Think about it. The cops in that town had you and Lady Blue, look where it got 'em. They lost the entire station house and there's one of their own, dead and an obvious pedophile. They now know what the fuck will happen to their town if they don't back off.

"What are they going to do, call ahead, admit how bad they fucked up, and then beg the military to protect the town for the next six years? No. They'll lick their wounds and try to pretend none of this ever happened.

"Now, it's time you learned something. The Chosen don't abandon their own, ever, that means you don't run out on us either. It's all sweet and nice that you want to take the heat off us, but that's not how it works. You chose to ride with us, and we chose to follow your lead."

"So, I'm stuck with you guys?"

"Damn right, you are."

"What about Ryder? You can't protect her and ..."

"Hey, lady," put in Ryder, "I just turned sixteen yesterday. I can make my own decisions. I owe you, and I owe these guys. My life's better now than ever before, and I swear I'll fight to the death rather than leave. If these guys want to ride with you, then I'm in, all the way."

Kara met her eyes then relented. "All right, but on one condition. Kyle has to give back my spark plug, or I'm not going anywhere."

When the laughter stopped, Kyle tossed her another beer and rose to go fix her bike.

Too Many Chances

They rolled into Seattle mid afternoon. "Well, someone's in a heap o' shit," roared a voice as they entered the biker bar, "the Chosen are in town."

"Hey, Mickey, how come you're still alive?" asked Thunder.

"Too ornery to die, I guess," replied the old bartender. "How about a round on the house for old time's sake?"

"You can't make a living that way, brother. The Chosen pay their way. Set 'em up."

The man started drawing glasses of beer. "So, who's all the new riders? Four new girls, you guys get broody or what?"

"This is the part where you mind your own business, Mickey."

"Sure. Thunder, you can't have them kids in here."

"Kids?" asked Kara, as she took a glass of beer from the bar. "Man likes to live dangerously, right Kyle?"

"Apparently so," chuckled Kyle.

Kara took a second beer and passed it to Ryder. "Kara," hissed Penny, "she's only sixteen, for god's sake."

"Seriously?" Kara turned to face Penny. "This woman is a warrior. She was a prisoner of war, held captive and tortured for years and survived, and you're freaking out because I gave her a fucking beer?"

"Hey, if that kid's only sixteen she can't be in here and she sure as hell can't have a beer. Jesus Christ, what the hell are you assholes thinking?"

Kara turned to face the bartender, her eyes cold as ice. "I'm thinking if you touch that alarm button you're a dead man. I'm thinking that this shit hole will be nothing but ashes by nightfall if you don't keep your mouth shut."

"So who the hell do you think ..." the man's voice trailed off. "Oh fuck, the news reports are right, aren't they? The Fallen Angel is riding with the Chosen. Thunder, are you guys crazy?"

Thunder snorted and took a second beer from the bar. "Use your head and keep your mouth shut, Mickey, or you're likely to see a whole new level of crazy."

The man's voice was shaky now. "Thunder ..."

"Just keep your head down and your mouth shut. You're old, don't see so good anymore. The ID looked good to you. You didn't see or hear anything out of the ordinary, right?"

Mickey sighed and nodded. "Am I going to get any older? Will I have a bar to come back to in the morning?"

"We're not here to cause trouble, Mickey. You know the kinds of things we do. You know what she's hunting. You got issues with that?"

"No, Thunder, I don't. Not a damn one. I just don't want to lose my bar, it's all I've got. That Asian girl, she's Lady Blue, isn't she? She's been all over news, too."

"Danged if I know," grinned Thunder, "just some stray who wanted to ride with us for a while. Seemed tough enough." Thunder winked at Mai then walked away to join Kara, Kyle, Penny, and Ryder at their table.

"Well, Ryder, what'd ya think?"

"I think this stuff tastes like shit," she replied, pushing the beer away.

"It's an acquired taste," grinned Kara.

"God, it's awful. Why do you drink so much of that?"

"Keeps me in a nasty mood."

"I can see how that would work. Can I have something else?"

"How about a ginger ale?" asked Penny, winking at Thunder.

"Sure."

"I'll have one too," said Penny, as she set her beer in front of Kara. She got up and went to the bar, bought the sodas then returned. She passed one to Ryder then looked around, puzzled. "Where'd Mai get to?"

"Said she had stuff to do," replied Kyle.

"Shit. That girl takes way too many chances. Gotta go."

Penny was on her feet when Kara's voice stopped her. "Want company?" she gazed into Kara's eyes for a moment then nodded. Grinning, Kara tossed down the last of her beer, wiped the foam from her mouth with her sleeve then jumped up and followed Penny out the door.

"So, where would she go? Any ideas?"

"One or two," replied Penny, as she ran at the side of a building and ran three strides up the side before turning in the air to grab the eave of the building next to it. She reached the roof with Kara close behind.

It was nearly an hour later they stopped to rest. "Are we there yet?" asked Kara, breathing deeply. "What the hell have you got against ground transportation anyway?"

"Too slow," replied Penny, her eyes scanning the busy streets below. "You're out of shape."

"Says you. So, what's the deal with the new girl. I thought she was created to help you bring me down. Won't happen."

"Don't flatter yourself. Mai was created for the same reasons we were, to push back the dark wherever we find it."

"So, she's my replacement?"

"Again with the self flattery. Mai's creation had nothing to do with you at all. She was already at work before you went renegade."

"Okay, so why is she tagging along with you then? You guys can't take me, you know that."

Penny sighed deeply and sat down with her back to a wall. "Kara honey, I'm not going to fight you, not ever. You're my sister, I love you, and I want you back. I want my soft-hearted, wise cracking, little sister back.

"That's why I'm here, that's why I'm following you around. It's like I told you, come back to us, embrace Moragah again, and I'll help you finish this hunt. We'll take down every damned pedophile we can find all across the country."

"But?"

"But we do it to save the kids, not for revenge. Please, Kara, at least think about it."

"Why does it matter so much?"

"Because revenge is a tool of the dark. By doing what you're doing you're bringing the dark closer to victory, the world closer to total destruction."

"And if we do it your way?"

"We push the dark back, bring hope where none existed before, increase the possibility of our world, our species' continued survival."

"Pretty speech, but ..."

Kara didn't get to finish the thought, as the sounds of battle reached their ears. A glance over the edge of the building showed Mai fighting a dozen men, street gang. Without another word, both avengers dropped from the roof and entered the brawl.

It wasn't a moment too soon as the gang's reinforcements came pouring out of an alley to join the fight. Kara grinned as she watched Mai in action. The girl was pretty, yet possessed of a deadly grace, and she was efficient, focused, lethal.

Penny, too, was efficient, but unlike Mai, she had no objection to using her guns. Kara, on the other hand was using blades. She was lightning quick, and utterly savage, maiming but not killing as she went.

When the battle finished Mai saw Kara approaching a number of the wounded. She watched in fascination as the tiny warrior approached, bloody knife in each hand. "Kara, what are you doing?" asked Penny.

"Dispatching the wounded. Never leave a live enemy behind."

"Don't do it." Mai's eyes went wide as Penny challenged Kara, something she'd been warned never to do.

Kara froze in place, a smile that was half sneer rested on her perfect features. "What did you say?"

"You heard me."

Kara's half smile turned to a wide grin. "Come on, Lady Blue, let me hear you say it." The voice in her mind was screaming at her now. "Go on, kill her, she's challenged you. No one can defeat you. Kill her."

At the sound of Penny voice, Kara clamped down hard on the demon on her shoulder. Her smile never wavered, nor did it reach her eyes. "Go on, Penny, say it."

Penny ground her teeth as she spoke. She had been so damn close, but, again the dark had stopped her from retrieving Kara, driven a wedge between them. If she was forced to fight, the darkness would have its win. She couldn't hope to defeat Kara. "Just drop the weapons and walk away, no harm will come to you."

Kara's grin widened as she straightened up to face Penny fully. "And if I don't?"

"We both have a really bad day."

Suddenly, to Penny's great surprise, Kara nodded and dropped her knives. "Okay, Lady Blue, I've dropped my weapons. Here's me, walking away." She turned, took two strides then blurred out of sight. She was in combat mode and gone before Penny could react.

Penny's shoulders slumped with relief. "Are we going after her?" asked Mai.

"Oh hell no," replied Penny as she turned and pulled Mai into a hug. "Thank Moragah you're all right." She kissed Mai's forehead then hugged her tighter again. "You take too many chances."

"I know," said Mai, as she returned Penny's hug then released her. "Come on, I hear the sirens getting closer. The bike's over here." She led the way and Penny got on behind her. They roared down the alley and onto the next street just as the first police car arrived followed closely by an ambulance.

"Where to?" asked Mai as they sped away.

"Back to the bar. I'm ready for that beer now."

The gang was still there when the girls returned. They sank into chairs at the table with Kyle, Ryder, and Thunder. Without a word Penny took Kyle's beer and drained it.

"Well, you two look like you've been busy," grinned Thunder. "Any of that blood yours?"

"Some, maybe," replied Mai. "Did Kara come back?"

"Not yet. What happened?"

"She let me live," sighed Penny. "That's what happened. We tracked Mai down and found her in a battle with a street gang. Just as we got there dozens more of them came pouring out of an alley. They had guns, knives, chucks, and all sorts of weapons.

"Jesus, Kara tore into them with just her knives, wounding but not killing so much. Once my guns were empty I used the knives, but she was so damned deadly. Once the last one was down, she was smiling as she started to kill them."

Kyle passed her another beer and she took a sip then went on. "She's just so damn strong. I had no real idea until today how strong she truly is."

"So, what happened?" asked Ryder. "Did she kill them after all?"

"No. She used the wounded to set me up, that's why she didn't kill them in the fight, she wanted them down, but alive. You see, I defend the weak, as does Mai, it's who we are, it's what we do.

"Kara trained with me for a long time, and she knows me, knows how I work. When she had them helpless she threatened them to force me to fight her. I was screwed and I knew it. I couldn't refuse, and I couldn't beat her.

"The demon in her head was already celebrating when she showed me how strong she really is. Kara knows I always do the same thing,

I have to. I always offer them a chance to walk away. Just drop the
weapons and walk away, and I'll let you go.

"She pushed me to it. I had no choice and was as good as dead, but
I saw her eyes shift. She fought that thing in her head, and she beat it.
Kara dropped her knives and walked away. I have no idea where she is
now, and I have no idea what she'll do next."

"I do," said Ryder, as she patted Penny's shaking hand. "She didn't
fight you because you're her sister, you're both Chosen. We fight for
each other, not against each other. Now she's out there, tracking down
the ones that hurt us and all the others. Tonight's payback time for
those fuckers, the Angel's coming for them."

"Yeah, you're probably right about that and there's not a damn
thing I can do to stop her."

"Do you even want to?"

Penny sighed again. "No, Ryder, I really don't."

Payback in Seattle

As darkness fell over the city the gang left for another bar, taking their time as they rode through the streets that only came alive when night fell. Penny and Mai went off on their own so they wouldn't be forced to interfere with the Chosen. They hunted on their own.

"So, how did you do it before?" asked Mai, as they sat on a rooftop, watching the street below.

"Do what?"

"Find the pedophiles?"

"I didn't. Tara had evidence of a ring where they moved the girls around. It was a big chain, and we never did locate the guy at the top, the one who owned it all, but she knew where to find the top guy in each city. We'd hit town and she'd go look him up while I found where the kids were being held.

"Once we had that, we'd bring them down and call a friend of hers in the FBI to come bust the boss if he was still alive." Penny was silent for a moment then went on.

"Sadly, in the end, some of those bosses managed to get off, others did a few months of time then got out. We both know they went back into business first chance they got. They can't help themselves."

"Excuse me?"

"They're not wired together right in the head. They can't help themselves. Something, the darkness inside, drives them to do what they do."

"So, you're saying there's only one way to make them stop."

"Yep, that's what I'm saying. I'm torn apart here, Mai, my sister. A piece of me really wants to let her go, to help her even, but I can't as long as she serves the darkness.

"Dammit, Mai, I almost had her this time. Two more minutes, that's all I needed. You couldn't wait, you just had to go back after that street gang."

"Sorry."

"The hell you are," sighed Penny, as she gently squeezed Mai's shoulder. "Can you tell me what that's all about?"

"They came from Asia years ago, landed in San Francisco, and like a poisonous infection, grew and spread. They came north when I was very small, bringing their violence and taking over all crime in the city. They grind the people under their feet, caring nothing for the lives they ruin.

"It wouldn't surprise me to find them behind your ring of pedophiles. To them, all women are simply slaves, a commodity to be used up and tossed aside. They eventually killed my father because he refused to bow down. They forced my mother into prostitution and me onto the streets when I was in my teens. The day I found her body was the day Moragah made me a priestess."

"So you hunt them?"

"No, I stop them from harming others, people on the street, small business people. I watch and when they attack, I stop them. However, I'm learning from Kara."

"Oh?"

"Yes. You were right, Penny. I hold back too much. Once the fight starts I should be more like Kara, just kill them as brutally and as quickly as possible. Take no chances."

Penny nodded then suddenly sat up straighter. Kara was on the street tossing a man around like a rag doll. Penny and Mai dropped to the pavement and approached. Kara was wearing the faceless mask. "Hey there, Fallen Angel, what's up?"

"Just chatting with the pimp here, but he's not playing fair."

"Oh?"

"He won't tell me what I want to know."

"Which is?"

"Where I find the pimp who sells the children."

"Hmm, mind if I ask him?"

"Fill your boots."

Penny turned to the man Kara had tossed to the pavement. "Hi there, Mr. Pimp. I recognized the Fallen Angel from the news descriptions. If they were that accurate, I'm sure they were pretty accurate about her methods too, right? So, here's the deal. If you hope to escape this with your life, you need to tell her what she wants to know."

"I can't. They'll kill me."

Penny's smile widened. "Now, you see, there's the rub. If you don't, she'll kill you, and I doubt it'll be quick or painless. She's right here, those other guys aren't, so here's what I suggest you do. Tell the lady what she wants to know, and then get in your car and run like hell, start a new life somewhere else."

He didn't respond, so Penny turned to Kara. "Well, I tried. Guess you'll have to do it your way. Later."

She turned away but had barely taken three steps before his voice stopped her. "All right, please, I'll talk. Please don't let her kill me." Penny turned back and the man started to babble. He broke down sobbing as he finished.

Mai had taken a small notebook from her pocket and written down everything he'd said. She passed the paper to Kara and pointed. "That way, about three blocks." Kara nodded then blurred out of sight. Penny was eyeing Mai. "What?"

Penny quirked an eyebrow at her. "You tell me."

"Two birds with one stone," replied Mai. "The man described is owned and controlled by the gang we fought earlier. We hurt them badly today and they'll be recruiting new muscle. Kara will now hurt them more while they're weak. Where's the bad?"

Penny grinned. "Good thinking, little sister."

"So, are we going to tag along to watch her back?"

"Nope. She forced me into making the challenge then let me off the hook. One thing I know for sure about Kara, don't push your luck with her."

"Okay, so what should we do?"

"We give her time to do her thing then we tie off any loose ends she leaves behind."

"We protect the agent of the darkness?"

"No, we finish off the damned pimps to make sure they can't start up again."

"The Asian gang will just recruit new ones."

Penny's shoulders sagged. "I know, Mai, but what else can we do? I'm wide open to suggestions here."

Mai sighed too and leaned her back against a wall. "Moragah said there will always be injustice in the world. Our task is not to defeat the dark, just to push it back to restore some balance. If we do as you say then we accomplish that task, buy the light some time.

"I believe you're right, Penny. There isn't a lot else we can do here."

"Thanks, Mai. We'll give her a bit more time then hunt up this guy she went after."

Mai nodded thoughtfully. "Do you think we can ever get her back?"

"Yeah, I do," said Penny, a wistful smile playing at her lips. "She's too strong for the dark to hold her. I know it wanted her to kill me this afternoon. I'd been maneuvered into a fight I didn't want, couldn't win.

"The dark set that up, but Kara saw the way out. She fought the demon and won. She can beat this thing and come back, but we have to give her a reason to want to. And we're going to have to be there when she does. She'll come out of it weakened and will need our support."

"And that will show her there's a real reason to stay?"

"Exactly."

"Okay, so, shall we take a stroll down the block and see what sort of trouble we can get into?"

"This is your city, Sister Mai. Lead on." They didn't find Kara's pimp. But they did find lots to keep them busy for the night.

———◉———

WHILE PENNY AND MAI were plotting strategy, the Fallen Angel had located her target. Her tactics were the same, follow the johns, make them pay, then return to the pimp to follow another one.

The thin balding man adjusted his glasses and sighed before downing another glass of whiskey. Across the room was a girl of about fourteen. She was naked and tied across a bench so her bare bottom was fully exposed.

Her wrists were shackled to her ankles and the backs of her legs glowed red from the paddling. She whimpered softly, waiting, knowing that more was coming. It came.

Outside a small figure dressed in black and wearing a faceless mask sat listening to the girl scream. The rage burned in her heart, but she forced herself to be patient. She had to be patient; it was the only way to get them all. The problem was how badly she wanted this one. This one was an old acquaintance.

At length the man untied the girl and told her to get dressed. He forced her to grovel and crawl up the stairs then out to the car in the driveway. She wasn't allowed to sit on the seat, but was put in the trunk for the ride back to the pimp.

He dropped her off at the meeting place and drove away, satiated at last for another month, perhaps more. The self loathing had set in, as he knew it would, by the time he reached home. Dammit, he had to stretch this out, he had to go longer between episodes. At least this time he had been able to rent one. He didn't have to kill her afterward.

Upon re-entering his house he stopped, thinking he heard a sound from the basement. There it was again, a girl crying, begging for mercy.

The devil rose up and took control of him again. Unable to stop himself, he descended the stairs and approached the dungeon. The door was open, but he was certain he had closed that.

Cautiously, he peered inside to hear a girl scream, begging him to stop. He recognized part of the action from two hours past. "Gets to you, doesn't it?" asked a soft feminine voice from behind him. He turned slowly, his eyes wide with fear. A small woman was behind him, her face a blank mask.

Fearfully, he backed away from her. "It's like a drug to you, isn't it?" she asked, as she closed the door then slowly advanced on him. As she reached the bench with the recorder on it, she shut it off, silencing the tortured screams of the child. "Answer me."

"Yes," he replied in a shaky voice.

"Can't stop yourself, can you?"

"No," he whimpered.

"Have you even tried?"

"Yes."

"Therapy?"

"No. Oh god no. Nobody must ever find out."

The woman stopped advancing. She pushed the mask back and shook out her hair then gave him a cruel smile. "See, there's the thing, I found out. Can you remember how?"

Recognition began to seep into his mind. It was her, the little blond who could take more pain than anyone else ever could. "Oh my god, it's you. You're the one they call the Fallen Angel. Please ..."

"Please what?"

"Please, Mistress, don't kill me."

"Well, since you asked so nicely, I'll consider it. Now, get your clothes off and bend over that bench." He didn't move, he just whimpered in fear. "You're just making it worse," she said as she picked up a whip.

The whip cracked right beside his face and he jumped back. "Get your clothes off and bend over that bench. It's gonna hurt a lot more if I have to do it for you." He quickly shed his clothes. Shaking with terror, he bent over the bench where just hours ago he'd had a girl child shackled.

He whimpered again as she fastened the wrist and ankle cuffs. "Now then," she said as she straightened up. "You've been a very bad boy, haven't you?"

"Yes mistress." He cringed as he felt the whip slide slowly down across his stretched hamstrings.

"Tell me, did you torture others while I was gone these past three years?"

"Yes." He screamed as the whip cracked across the back of his legs.

"What was that?"

"Yes, Mistress. Yes Mistress."

"How many?"

"I don't know ..."

The whip cracked again bringing another scream. "Try again."

"Eleven. It was eleven, Mistress. Please."

"Did you hire them all from the pimp like you did me, or did you go out and capture some on your own."

Her only answer was a soft sob. The whip sang again and he jerked violently as he screamed. "Yes, Mistress. Yes."

"How many?"

"Four, Mistress."

"Did you kill them or sell them to the pimps?" Again no answer. She swung the whip higher so it struck his exposed genitals as well as his legs. When the screaming stopped he sobbed out a confession. "I killed them, Mistress."

"Why? Why not sell them?"

"The pimps won't buy local meat, Mistress." He screamed again as the blow fell.

"Meat? That's what you used to call me, wasn't it?"

"Yes, Mistress."

She tossed aside the whip where he could see it. He trembled as she took up the leather paddle and showed it to him. "All right, Mr. Bad Boy, Tell me what you think a fitting punishment should be for hurting those eleven children?"

"The paddle, Mistress," he sobbed.

"The paddle, good idea. The paddle it is. So, you had me in this room seven times, that's seven strokes with the paddle, then there's eleven more for the others, and we'll add two each for the ones you killed. Does that sound fair?"

"Yes Mistress."

"So, that's twenty-six in all. You count them. If you lose count, we'll start over. Ready?"

"Yes, Mistress," he whimpered. The whimper was followed by a scream of pain as the paddle struck low just above the knees.

"I said count them," she snarled as she struck again.

"Two," he sobbed as he stopped screaming.

"Wrong. We start over."

This time the leather landed on the small of his back bringing a howl of pain. "One," he sobbed.

He managed to keep the count until she stopped at seven. "Okay, good boy. So, that's all for me. Now we go for the others. Ready?"

"Mistress, please ..." he screamed in pain again as the leather hit his genitals. "Eight."

Slap! "Nine."

"So tell me about them."

"Mistress?"

"The ones you killed after you tortured them." Slap!

"Ten," he gasped when he got his breath back. "The first one was younger. She didn't last long." Splat!

"Eleven, eleven, oh god, please Mistress ..." Slap! "Twelve, twelve." He hung across the bench sobbing.

"Tell me about the second one."

"Please. I didn't want to, but the first one was no good, I had to get an older one."

"Older?"

"Yes, at least ten or twelve."

"Let me get this straight, the first one was too young, so you took another?"

His reply was so soft she barely heard it. "Yes Mistress."

With a snarl she leaped at him. The paddle struck with power four times in rapid succession. "Count," she demanded.

The answer came between sobs. "Thirteen, fourteen, fifteen, sixteen." Another four strokes came in rapid succession. When he stopped screaming he sobbed out the count. "Seventeen, eighteen, nineteen, twenty."

"Tell me about the next one you killed."

"She was a pretty child with hair like yours, Mistress."

"And the last one?"

"An Asian girl."

"When was that?"

"Mistress, please ..."

"When?"

"A few weeks ago. Please ..."

"Where are the bodies?"

He didn't answer at first, just sobbed in pain and defeat. "They're out back, Mistress, under the roses."

The paddle rose and fell in swift succession four times. When he stopped screaming he managed to sob out the count. "Twenty-one, twenty-two, twenty-three, twenty-four."

He hung over the bench sobbing. Horror set in as he realized she had recorded the whole thing. He craned his neck around and with wide eyes watched as she picked up the recorder and re-set it to the start.

"This is the Fallen Angel. My message is for whatever police officer finds this. Listen carefully to the whole recording, there's important information for you at every step."

She shut it off then approached, the paddle struck twice again.

"Twenty five, twenty six," he sobbed.

The angel knelt down by his head. He was whimpering, weeping, and begging for mercy. "Hush now," she said as she caressed his head, "you've been a good boy and now it's time for your reward." A quick twist of her hands and his neck snapped.

She stood and walked away, leaving his dead body hanging over the bench he had so often used to torture her.

———◉———

IT WAS JUST PAST NOON the next day, a few of the Chosen, including the Ladies Blue, were in a coffee shop, soaking up some caffeine. Thunder, Penny, and Ryder were at one table. A policeman entered, bought a coffee then pulled up a chair and sat with them. Mai stood and slipped out the back door.

All was silent at the table while the officer took a long pull from the steaming mug. Finally he spoke. "When you see Lady Blue again tell her I saw her go out the back and I don't give a shit."

Nobody responded to that so he went on. "Look, we know the Fallen Angel rides with the Chosen."

"Angels don't ride with the Chosen," rumbled Thunder. "Chosen don't ride with the Angels. That's just how it is."

"Right."

"Was there something important you wanted to talk about, or did you just want to hang out?"

The policeman took another long sip from his coffee. "Last night we got a call from some folks who noticed their neighbor's door open and flapping in the wind. His car was home, but the lights weren't on. They called us and we investigated."

Thunder nodded slowly, fighting the grin that tried to claim him. "Find anything interesting?"

Penny noticed the man's hands trembling as he gripped the coffee mug tightly and replied. "We did. The house belonged to a suspected pedophile. We found him in his own torture chamber, his naked and tortured body draped across a bench and lashed down."

Thunder just nodded, so the cop went on. "We also found a recording device. The Fallen Angel had tortured and killed him, and she'd recorded the whole thing."

"Ah-huh."

"That recording was hard to hear, biker. It's not easy to listen to a man scream like that."

"She must have had a reason," said a soft voice.

The policeman turned his attention to Ryder. "She did, girl. She tortured that animal to make him confess, confess how many girls about your age he'd had in that room. She also made him confess how he'd captured, and killed, local girls. When the pimps didn't have any suitable hookers or captives for him, he'd snatch locals.

"Jesus Christ, she made him confess then made him tell where he hid the bodies. She only learned about four, but so far we've found eighteen bodies in that back yard and we're still looking.

"Christ, I just wish I knew why she let him torture that kid before she took him down."

"She had to," said Ryder. "She had no choice."

"Excuse me?"

Ryder finally looked up and met his gaze. "It's how she finds them. She locates a pimp who provides young girls, and then she follows a john home. She waits until he's finished and takes the girl back. When he comes home again is when she takes him down. If she rescues the girl she loses the trail. She can follow a single girl to a dozen freaks or more."

"And you know this because?"

"I was the last one the pimp had the night she took him. I was sold by my foster father when I was twelve. Eventually the Angel finished off every damn one of the men who hurt me, then let me watch when she killed the pimp. I had no family so she left me with these guys."

"Jesus, kid. Look, I can take you in, get a statement, then make damn sure you get placed somewhere safe. I ..."

"No fucking way in hell," said Ryder, as she pushed back in her chair. "My mother got herself jailed and I was tossed around through your mighty system for a few years until I was slaved out.

"The Angel brought me to the Chosen. They don't ask anything of me, they don't do anything to me, and any one of them would die trying to protect me. I swear I'd do the same for any one of them. Fuck you and your system. I'm Chosen, I ride with my brothers and sisters."

The big cop just nodded. His hands were still shaking, but his coffee cup was empty. Penny took it from his hand and went for a refill. No one spoke until she returned.

He gave her a sheepish smile as she put the now full mug in his hands. He took a sip then returned his attention to Ryder. "All right, kid. As far as I'm concerned you're twenty-eight and can make your own damn decisions. I also accept that your story happened ten years ago, waste of time to pursue it now."

The man's hands were still shaking and he was clearly fighting strong emotions. Penny reached over and gently patted his hand. "Officer, why did you come to us with this?"

He gave her a nod of thanks then sighed. "Three years ago my sister's daughter disappeared. We never found a trace of her."

"And you're afraid she's in that back yard."

"No, I'm praying she's not, because if she's not then she might still be alive. It would kill me to think she was the one screaming on that recording and I couldn't help her. Sadly, if she is there, at least my family will get some closure, but I'll never dare tell them about the torture or the screams."

"I get that," said Thunder. "Can't talk to the fellow officers either, I'll bet."

"No, I can't. They wouldn't understand."

"That you want the Fallen Angel to run free?" asked Ryder.

"Very astute, kid. Yeah, that."

"So, what's her name?"

"What?"

"The girl's name, what is it?" asked Thunder. "You know, just in case I ever do run into this Fallen Angel, I can pass it along."

The policeman gazed into Thunder's eyes for a long moment then took out his card and wrote a name plus his personal number on the back of it. He pushed it across the table and Thunder put it in his jacket pocket. "Now, I have one for you, officer."

"Oh?" The man was instantly wary.

"Ever hear of a man named Merle Downy?"

"No, can't say that I have. Why?"

"Old Merle is a procurer."

"Procurer?"

"He captures the girls, trains them himself, and then sells them to the pimps. That somebody we've never heard of is on his trail," replied Thunder.

The big officer nodded slowly. "Okay, if I ever run across this man, can I get a message to you? Without evidence we'd have no reason to hold him, so ..."

"Mickey's Bar on East Tenth, old Mickey tends the bar himself. Just tell him the lost has been found. The message is for Thunder."

"Thunder, that's you?"

"It is."

"I'm not even going to ask."

"Thanks for that."

The officer chuckled, bringing the first smile to his face. "Okay, back to work for me. We never had this conversation." He stood up and squared his shoulders. He spoke again in a loud voice. "That's pure bullshit, biker. Just keep your nose clean while you're in town." He winked at Ryder then walked out the door.

"What the hell just happened here?" asked Ryder.

"That's easy, girl," Thunder replied. "The man's hurting, and what he found last night tore the scab off an old wound. If they don't find his niece, then she could still be out there. Thing is, under the law, he could end up having to protect the man who took her."

"So he wants Kara to do the nasty for him."

"Pretty much, but what else could he do?"

"He could quit his bullshit job and go after her himself. All the girls cry for their dads or uncles to come save them, but nobody ever does."

"Easy, Ryder, easy," said Penny, as she patted the girl's hand. "It's not the man's fault. He probably didn't even know about this crap happening until today. Now he's blaming himself for not getting her back. He's not the bad guy, Ryder."

"She's right, kid," sighed Thunder. "The bad guy is somebody like that piece of shit Angel finished off last night. That's why Blue and Kara do the things they do."

"So why are you trying to stop her?" Ryder's eyes were hard as she glared at Penny.

"I'm not trying to stop her, Ryder, I'm just trying to change her motivation. Right now she's doing it for revenge. That's the work of the darkness, and it'll just bring more people like the one she killed into being. I want her to do it to rescue the kids. I swear, if she'll come back to me, I'll help her finish the lot of them."

"Why would you? What difference does it make?"

"Saving the kids is the work of the light. That'll push back the dark and hopefully thin out these kinds of people."

"Yeah, then why aren't you out there ahead of her. Do the job the right way so she can't do it wrong?"

"I thought of that, but if I try she'll just head for another city and I'll lose contact, lose my chance to get my sister back."

The girl was thoughtful for a moment then she reached out and gently squeezed Penny's hand. "That makes sense. I wish I'd had a sister like you, somebody who'd go to the wall for me no matter what. I do now, and I can see the difference. I hope she listens to you."

She patted Penny's hand again then went back to staring at her coffee. "Thunder, can you tell me why it's such a fucking big deal if I have a beer, but I can have as much of this rot gut as I want?"

"I have no idea at all," he grinned, winking at Penny. "Doesn't make any sense, does it?"

Just then Kyle returned and dropped a small bag in front of Ryder. "What's this?"

"Your new ID." He bought a mug of coffee and joined them.

Ryder was looking the identification. It looked enough like her at first glance. Could work. "Where'd you get this?"

"Bought it off a junkie downtown. She said the bank card's bogus, but the DL and birth certificate are real. The credit card's maxed out and the company is after her for the money, so don't try to use it."

"Kyle, why did you do this?"

"So now there'll be no fuss when we go to a bar. We go in, you show that, then we have a beer."

"This'll cover me for driving a bike too, won't it."

"Yup, it will."

"Cool. Kyle, you're the best. Do I get my colors now?"

"Sure," he replied with a grin. "Come on."

Penny and Thunder watched them go. "What's that grin for, Blue?"

"I was just thinking, in spite of the bad shit Kara's doing, the dark still doesn't have full control of her. She's still doing some good where she can. She saw how tough that girl is, and rather than abandon her, or send her back to the system, she sent her to you guys, a place where she could find herself again.

"Ryder's been too badly abused, Thunder. She could never find a place in normal society, but with the Chosen, she can make a good life."

Thunder nodded thoughtfully. "So, you're saying we're not normal."

"Oh hell no, not even close," grinned Penny. He gave a great bellowing laugh then went for a refill on the coffee.

Outside, Ryder struggled as she fought to right the huge bike Kyle had laid down on its side. She knew she had to get it back up and on the kickstand before he'd teach her how to drive it. It was a real battle, but with a final grunt of victory she stood it up and applied the kickstand.

With a wide grin of true delight she ignored the scrape on her shin and faced him. "Well done, little sister," he grinned as he passed back her leather jacket. It had a big blue spiral on it.

They heard applause as she put it on and danced around. There was Kara, clapping her hands and grinning with delight. "Nicely done, Ryder, nicely done."

"It's like you told me, never quit, no matter how damn hard it gets, just keep going."

"I'm proud of you, girl," said Kara, as she gave the girl a hug. "So, Kyle, you the teacher today?"

"Yup, that's me. She's earned it, Angel."

"Damned right she has, that and then some. The others inside?"

"Blue's there with Thunder. I think the other cutie skipped out when the cop showed up."

"The cop? He still in there?"

"Nope."

"What'd he want?"

"Damned if I know, I followed Mai out the back door. Had an errand to run, if you know what I mean."

Kara grinned. "You're teaching her to ride. That mean you got her some ID?"

"Ah-huh, that I did. I'll be careful with her, Angel, teach her to ride right."

"Then you're forgiven for stealing my spark plug." He grinned at that. "Kyle?"

"Yeah?"

"Don't ever do that again." He was still chuckling as she walked inside and ordered coffee.

Kara took her coffee and sat with Penny and Thunder. "So, I heard you had a visitor."

"That we did," replied Thunder. "Seems like you had a busy night."

She nodded at that. "He say anything interesting?"

"He said they've found eighteen bodies in that backyard so far," said Penny.

"Damn," said Kara as she set her coffee back down and held the mug in both hands. "Double damn. He say anything else?"

Thunder nodded. "He said his niece disappeared a couple of years ago. He's praying she's not in that backyard."

"Aw, shit," sighed Kara. "Yeah, I'll bet that bastard's been at this for a long time. Anything else?"

"He said he'd keep an eye out for Merle Downy," replied Thunder, as he slid the policeman's card across the table to her.

"This him?" she asked, as she studied the card.

"Yup, it is."

"And this would be the girl's name and his number, right?"

Again Thunder nodded. "Said we'd keep an eye out just in case." She nodded and slipped the card into her pocket.

Cleaning House

The gang was camped outside the city limits that night. Penny was with them, but Mai was hunting and so was the Fallen Angel. Penny was praying they didn't bump into each other. Since Penny had no plans to get in Kara's way, Mai went back to her old haunts.

Staring into the fire, Penny called to Moragah. *I am here, my priestess."*

"Moragah, it's been weeks now and I've been so close. Is there any hope at all?"

"There is always hope, Penny, my daughter, and now there is greater hope. You must keep trying. Just having you near is weakening the dark's hold on Kara. She refused to fight you once you had been forced to make the challenge. The darkness is beginning to fear her now, for it now knows she is the stronger.

"Even as she gives in to the darkness inside her and seeks revenge, she still finds ways to push back, to bring some good from what she is doing. Penny, even now she seeks the policeman's niece.

"Every day Kara moves a bit farther from the darkness. Keep trying, Penny. You must keep trying. She will come back to us, and she will need you there when she does for the power needed to break free from the darkness could destroy her."

"Moragah?"

"We dare not let the darkness keep her, Penny. We must get her back. Keep showing her the light, keep the good things she's done before her."

"You mean like Ryder."

"Yes, that young woman may yet be the catalyst that breaks the dark's grip on Kara's heart. Be patient, Penny. I have every faith that you will

succeed." With that Moragah pulled back, sending a wave of warm loving energy through Penny.

"You okay, Blue?"

"Huh? Oh, yeah, Ryder, I'm good. How are the riding lessons going?"

The girl grinned broadly and fairly danced with excitement. "Awesome, so awesome. I drove all the way out of the city with Kyle on the back and he only screamed like a girl twice."

"Hey, now," said Kyle, shaking a warning finger at Ryder while Penny howled with laughter.

Ryder sat beside Penny and passed her a bottle of water. "You're not following her tonight?"

"Nope. Listening to that policeman this morning bummed me out. She's cleaning house on this town and I'm not inclined to interfere. Dammit, I was so close to getting her back before that brawl with the Asian gang. Now I have to start over."

"Anything I can do to help?"

"You want to help me?"

"Yeah, I do. I thought about what you said, about the difference, the reason for doing the things you do. Kyle told me how the Chosen got its name, the way you challenged the guys to do the same stuff but for a better reason. I think you're right about this.

"Besides, if you can bring her back then the two of you working together could help a lot of people like me."

"Yes we could, but I know what she does to find the johns and I don't know if I could do that."

"Sure you could, Blue. You'd just have to toughen up a bit."

"What? Why you little ..." Ryder giggled and cringed away as Penny ruffled her hair. "Actually, there is something you can do to help, Ryder."

"Uh, yeah?"

"Kara looks to you as a little sister. You both went through hell and have a special bond. Keep that going, Ryder. It'll help more than you know."

"Yeah, she's cool and really good to me. What's she like when she not the evil angel?"

Penny smiled at that. "Kara's still tough as nails, no worries about that. She's always up for a challenge, and she's always wise cracking. Kara always has a comeback. You saw some of that when Kyle took one of the spark plugs from her bike.

"In spite of what was done to her, she's all heart. The girl has a lot of love to give, but she's also got trust issues. You know what that's all about. She's fiercely protective of the few folks she calls friends and she loves gentle, fun, teasing."

"Gentle, fun, teasing?"

"Like Kyle taking the spark plug. There was nothing mean in it, no name calling, no nasty sarcasm, just a silly way to make her stop and listen."

"Okay, I get it. She's been hurt enough, and teasing that was hurtful would piss her off. Got it, makes perfect sense. Penny, nobody in the Chosen would do anything to hurt her."

"I know. That's why I'm so thrilled she hooked up with these guys. They won't hurt her, they make her feel safe."

"That's why she brought me to them, she knew they'd keep me safe."

"Ah-huh."

"Can I tell you something?"

"She gave you the gun and let you kill the pimp?"

"No. She let me use the whip on him, but she shot him. No, it's just how bad I wanted to do it. Does that make me a tool of the darkness too?"

Penny put her arm around the girl's shoulders. "No, girl, it just makes you someone who was hurt too much too often. I'd have felt the same." She gave the girl a gentle squeeze then released her.

———◆———

IN A SEEDY PART OF town two men argued angrily. "I don't give a shit what you want, asshole, I told you I ain't gonna pay it, not for this trash. You and I both know the Fallen Angel's in town, cleaning out your customer base. You have to feed this lot and you're not making any money. Everybody's too scared to buy right now."

"Yeah, well too bad for you, cheapskate. Not gonna happen, no discounts, no deals. You either pay the going rate or you go home and beat your own ass. This is quality merchandise, the best in the city right now. Besides, aren't you afraid the angel will find you too?"

"She can't find me. Unlike the rest of these nitwits, I'm really damn careful on the internet. I only check the real sites from the work computer, and I'm never there except in daylight. The angel's like a fucking vampire, she only hunts in the dark."

"You sure about that?" asked a soft feminine voice. Both men whipped around to see a small figure moving in the shadows. They both pulled out guns, but she was already in combat mode. Their guns were batted aside and they were knocked to the floor.

Both men quivered in fear, she was standing over them, a gun in each hand. She stepped back and tucked one gun into her belt then pushed the mask up so they could see her face. They both recognized her. As that recognition reached their eyes she fired. Both men lay dead on the floor.

"Now, let's see what we've got here." Kara began to go through their pockets. She got a wad of cash from the john and a bigger wad of cash from the pimp, plus a cell phone and a bonus. On her third try she got the phone's password. "Slut, these guys have no real imagination at all. Now, let's see what we've got here."

It took her a few minutes, but she found the list under reminders. "Contact john seven, contact john nine ... What the hell?" she checked the man's pockets again and turned up a small address book. There was the golden list.

Each name and address was assigned a john number and a date for a monthly payment. "So, you're not just an ordinary scumbag of a pimp, you're a blackmailer too. Okay, where would you keep the evidence, somewhere close? I'll bet you do."

She began to search the place. Suddenly there was a soft tentative voice. "Master? Are you there?"

"He's dead. You guys in the room with the padlock on it?"

"Yes. Are you going to kill us?"

"Nope. I'll let you out of there in a minute or two. Just be patient now." She continued her search. "Dammit, if I was a dumbass pimp, where would I hide something super important around here? Naw, could you really be that much of an asshat?"

She stepped to the door where the girls were captive and ripped the lock away. "Hi kids, you okay?"

"Yes, who are you?"

"They call me the Fallen Angel."

They all began to cower and cry. "Please don't kill us, please ..."

"Hey, hey, I'm not going to hurt you guys. What made you think I'd do a thing like that?"

"Master said you kill people like us, that we had to be super quiet so you wouldn't be able to find us."

"Master was a lying piece of shit. I kill people like him, him and the johns. Girl, I used to be one of you. Now I'm killing all the johns."

"You're killing the masters?"

"I am. Every damn one of them who put a whip to my ass will die by my hand. I'd never hurt one of you guys. Now, tell me, did that moron keep anything secret in here?"

"No, just the list of clients. That's what he calls the johns."

"Where is it?"

The girl carefully rose from the floor where she cowered and went to the wall. She slid aside a panel and there was a file cabinet. Kara took a quick look and nearly puked at the pictures. All the blackmail evidence was there. "Dirty rotten son of a bitch.

"All right, guys, I'm going to call the cops to come and get you. They'll help you get home."

"You mean it, we get to go home?"

"Yeah, the cops will help you. When they get here, show them this file cabinet, okay?"

"Okay. Will you stay with us?"

"Sorry, sis, but I've got more work to do tonight."

"You're going to go kill more of the johns, aren't you?"

"Yes ma'am, that's exactly what I'm going to do. Any of you named Grace? No? Okay, you guys relax now and I'll call the cops." Kara pulled out the policeman's card and called the number.

"Who the hell is this and how did you get this number?"

"I'm the Fallen Angel and I got the number from a friend. I'm using a dead pimp's phone. Now, officer, pay attention, I'm going to give you an address. There you'll find the dead pimp, a dead john, and a bunch of badly abused kids."

Her voice dropped into a softer tone. "I'm really sorry, officer, the girl you're looking for isn't here, but I'll keep an eye out. Now, here's where you find them ..."

She gave him the address then broke the connection. He called out to his partner and as soon as she was in the car he set out with the lights on and the siren howling. When he arrived he found things exactly as she'd said he would.

In a darkened room a man sat sipping his favorite whiskey, and listening to the music of a woman's screams. Lights flickered across the excitement on his face as the recording played out across the screen. He smiled with delight and the memories, but in the shadows a white hot rage burned.

Something whizzed past his head and smashed the huge TV screen. Startled he leaped to his feet. The lights came up and he was looking at the girl who had just been on the screen. She was holding a huge knife and she didn't look happy. He smirked as he saw who it was.

"Well, well, well, look who's come home to daddy. Drop that knife, slave." Trembling, she dropped it. "Now, get on your fucking knees and crawl over here to your master."

A cruel smile reached her lips and death danced in her eyes. "I've got a better idea." Her voice suddenly changed and sounded like a demon from hell. "You get on your knees and crawl over here to your mistress."

Whimpering in fear and sweating with the effort to resist her, he none-the-less slowly dropped to his knees and began crawling to her. Terrified, he watched her pick up the knife again. As he reached her he heard that voice again.

"Stay on your knees. Now, hold your head up. Good, now I'm going to cut your head off and stick it on the gate out front, a warning to all the other bastards like you that I'm coming for them."

He trembled in fear and wept, begging her not to kill him as he felt the cold steel of the knife gently caress his neck. "I used to ask you for mercy. Do you remember what you used to tell me? I do."

Her finger gripped his hair and her muscles bunched. In a single pass the head was severed from the shoulders. Blood spurted everywhere and she held the head at arm's length until it stopped.

With a snarl of pure hate she turned and strode to the front door then kicked it open. She walked to the end of the driveway and stuck the head on the spike of the gate then blurred onto combat mode and disappeared.

It was nearly dawn when the homeless man found a small girl asleep on a pile of cardboard behind a dumpster. He smiled sadly and covered her with his ragged blanket then walked away. It was close to noon when she awakened.

Kara rose, stretched, then squatted behind the dumpster to relief herself. Feeling better, but hungry, she left the alley and found a homeless man sitting in the sun. "Hey there, was that your blanket I borrowed?" he grinned and nodded.

"I appreciate that, brother. Can I buy you breakfast?"

"Sure."

"Let's go." She passed back the blanket and helped him up. "Where to?"

"That way. They won't let me in there, but you could bring something out."

"Works for me." They reached the coffee shop and she bought two breakfasts to go. She sat with her new buddy and enjoyed the sun and the meal.

"You're that girl on the TV. We're supposed to call the cops if we see you."

"That right? You got a TV in your pocket?"

"Nooo, silly. I go watch through the window of the store. They always chase me away, but I sneak back."

"Cool. So, are you going to call the cops?"

"Nope, can't," he replied with a sloppy grin. "I got no phone."

He laughed at his own joke and she grinned. "Thanks, brother." She tucked a wad of cash into his pocket. "There's a bit of money. Get yourself a better blanket and a meal."

"Hey, thanks," he replied, as she rose to go.

"Thank you for tucking me in last night." She blurred onto combat mode and disappeared.

A man who'd just stepped out of the cafe nearly went into shock. "That woman, that woman just disappeared. Did you see that?"

"Yeah, I saw her. She's an angel, and she bought me breakfast." He grinned as he dumped the garbage into the receptacle on the curb then ambled away.

It was nearly dark again when Kara joined the Chosen at a bar. First thing she noticed was Adam with his arm in a sling. She nodded and sat with Penny, Mai, Ryder, and Thunder. "What happened to him?" she asked as she sat and took a sip from her beer.

"We were discussing politics with a pimp," grinned Thunder. "One of the hookers whipped out a gun and shot him."

"She still alive?"

"Oh yeah, but she's got one hell of a shiner."

"Oh?"

"Yeah," grinned Thunder. "Ryder decked her. Girl's got a wicked left hook."

Kara laughed with delight and gave Ryder a fist bump. "All right, my sister."

Ryder just beamed her delight at Kara's approval.

"So, you've been busy," said Mai. "What's with the idea of the guy's head on a spike?"

Kara, just studied her hands for a minute. "Yeah, that was bad form all right." She sighed and raised her head to meet Mai's gaze. "I found the guy and he was watching home movies."

"Home movies?"

"Of him taking a whip to my bare ass and laughing while I screamed. I lost it all over him and stuck his head on the fence."

Nobody spoke for a moment. "Good job," said Ryder. "I recognized the guy when they showed his face on the TV. Bastard got off easy."

Penny sighed then gently laid her hand on Kara's arm. "Kara ..."

"Penny, don't even start."

"No, sis, I understand, I do. I can't even imagine what that must have done to you, seeing that. I just wanted to say thanks for saving that bunch of kids. That was well done."

"Yeah, I guess," replied Kara, giving Penny a small grin. "So, Ryder, where did that left hook come from?"

"Marla's been teaching me."

"Kung Fu?" asked Mai.

"Don't know. She just offered to show me how to fight dirty and win."

"She'd be the one who knows about that," grinned Thunder. "Marla's a real hellcat in a brawl. So, we done here in Seattle?"

"Not yet. I've got a few more on the list."

"You've got a list?" asked Penny.

"Yeah. The pimp I shut down was a blackmailer too," replied Kara. "He had a list and an address book in his pocket. The kids showed me where he kept the evidence. I left it for the cops."

"Marty, the fucking scumbag," snarled Ryder.

"You knew that guy, Ryder?"

"Yeah, Angel, I did, the evil bastard. He dead?"

"As a doornail."

"Awesome. Justice is served."

"Ryder, is there anybody else I should know about?"

"Probably lots. We haven't been to Portland yet, Vancouver either."

Kara sighed and drained her beer. "Yeah, it's still a work in progress." She turned to Penny. "You mad at me?"

"Nope."

"But you're still going to nag me."

"Of course, I'm your big sister, aren't I?" Kara just grinned shyly, and Penny allowed herself a glimmer of hope.

"Doesn't it ever bother you, killing all those people?" asked Mai. Penny gave her a hard look, but she didn't notice.

"It used to," replied Kara, "but not anymore."

"Not since you went over to the dark."

"That would be it, yeah."

"Now you enjoy it."

Too late, Mai realized she'd pushed too hard. Kara turned to her with hellfire and death dancing in her eyes. "Is that what you think, pretty girl? You think I do what I do for fun? You have no fucking idea what it's like.

"I kill these scummy bastards because they tortured and raped me, because they tortured and raped her, and because they'll never fucking stop until somebody has the guts to stop them. I don't kill for fun; I don't get a cheap thrill from it like they did from whipping me. I do it to make them stop, period.

"Once I'm done, they never whip another kid, ever. That's why I do it. Now shut the fuck up and get out of my face."

Mai had fear in her eyes as she looked to Penny. Penny jerked her head at the door and Mai left. "She didn't mean anything by it, Kara."

"The hell she didn't."

"She just has no idea what you went through, what they all went through."

"No she doesn't, Penny, but she might if you got off your ass and took her out hunting once in a while."

"Is that what you want, Kara?"

"Yes it is. That girl has no fucking idea, and she never will unless somebody educates her. You damn well better hope it's not me who does it."

"Give me your list."

"What?"

"You want me to go hunting, give me the list."

Kara gazed into Penny's eyes for a long moment then relented. She took out the address book and tore out a page. "Two pages left, Penny. One each. You gotta do it all. It's not enough to just free the kids, they'll just start up again."

Penny nodded as she took the torn page. "I know, Kara. I'll do it right, for the kids and for you." Kara broke the gaze and turned her attention to the beer that had magically appeared before her.

Penny made eye contact with Ryder, nodded at Kara, then when she was sure the girl understood, she turned and left the bar. Mai was waiting by the motorcycle outside. "Penny, I'm sorry."

"Not yet you're not, but you will be. Kara gave me her list. We're going hunting tonight."

Getting an Education

Mai trembled with outrage and the desire to do something, anything to stop the girl's screaming. Penny's iron grip on her wrist held her back. They had checked out the addresses on the list then began watching. This was the third night, the first two were quiet, but not now.

"Penny ..."

"No," ground out Lady Blue, "Not yet. Just shut up and listen." Tears of frustration and compassion ran down Mai's face as she listened to the slap of the whip on flesh.

She bit into her own lip as she heard the man's cruel laughter when he explained to his victim that he was changing from the whip to the bamboo cane. The screams began again. "Penny, please ..."

"This was Kara's life for three years. Ryder, too, Mai. You need to know and understand."

"I was trying to understand ..."

"You were judging, Mai. Yes, you were trying to understand too, so here we are. Now you get it, now you understand Kara."

"Yeah, I get it. I'm gonna kill that man but I'm giving him pain first."

"He's all yours, Mai, but first we follow him back to where the girls are kept."

"Then we kill the pimp, too, please?"

"Then we kill the pimp, too. Okay, sounds like he's finishing up."

They were listening to the child's sobbing as she was raped. Mai ground her teeth in frustrated rage. She'd thought she'd seen the depths to which humans could sink, but this night had been an education, an education she could have happily lived without.

Finally the man came out and roughly shoved the girl into his car. He drove away blissfully unaware of the blacked out motorcycle following him. He dropped her off in a rough part of town.

"Mai, can you remember this place?"

"Sure."

"Okay, get us back to his house. It's time for this scum to face the music." The motorcycle turned and raced away.

The man returned home and sighed with satisfaction. He was inside with the door locked before he sensed something was wrong. The basement lights were on. Fearfully he turned and ran towards the door, but a woman was there. She pointed at the basement stairs.

He didn't move, so she grabbed him and threw him down the stairs. Another woman was there, waiting for him. She had a whip in her hand and was pointing at the torture room. He didn't move fast enough and the whip in her hand cracked.

He screamed in pain as the whip bit through his shirt and drew blood on his back. His body jerked forward involuntarily as the whip struck a second time. "Please stop. Who are you people?"

The whip struck again, then the girl tossed it aside. The blond arrived and picked it up. He trembled in fear as she approached. "You're a lucky man, scumbag."

"I am?"

"You were on our sister's list. She'd be really mean to you, hell, she'd probably skin you alive."

"I might anyway," said the Asian girl, as she picked up his favorite bamboo cane.

"No, please, no ..." His pleas fell on deaf ears and turned into a scream as she struck.

"Stand up," she commanded.

"No, please, don't ..."

"Oh, fuck it," she snarled, as she suddenly grabbed him and hauled him to his feet. A single stiff fingered blow to the throat crushed his larynx and sent him crashing back to the floor, gagging and desperately fighting to draw breath, and failing.

As the man choked out his life he heard her ask the blond, "Do we still have time to catch another one tonight?"

"No, we're done for now," replied Penny as she kicked aside the body and headed for the stairs. "We'll rest, then go back out later, now we find a place to crash for a few hours."

Mai drove them to a parking lot then they took to the roof tops. A short run later they reached a small apartment building that looked abandoned. One of the top apartments had an odd lived in feel. "Your secret hideaway?"

Mai grinned shyly. "Yeah. Our place when my father was still alive. I hide out here from time to time."

"Cool."

"Penny."

"Yeah?"

"I don't know whether to thank you or shoot you for tonight. My god, it ..." she broke down and Penny held her gently until the storm of emotion passed. "Didn't that have any effect on you at all?"

Penny gave her another gentle squeeze then released her. "Mai, the first time I encountered this crap I puked for days every time I thought of it. My partner and I went on the hunt, but we were just shutting it down wherever we found it. I killed a few of the pimps and such, but we never went after the johns. It didn't really occur to me.

"Anyway, we were working in Portland when we found Kara and brought her out. We'd met her grandfather by accident and so there was a connection there. Eventually, Moragah made her a priestess and I trained her.

"Mai, I have no idea at all what triggered the dark rage in her, broke her iron grip on it, but I understand where it comes from. They had her for over three years, years when she should have been home with her family, going to school, having boyfriends, etc.

"Instead she was moved around the country, used and abused by men like that. What was done had to burn deep."

"You're right. God, it's no wonder she went on the warpath. Oh god, I have so misjudged Kara. Do you think I can ever make it right with her?"

"Yeah, you can. As soon as we finish our part of the list we'll reconnect. It'll be different then."

"But we still have to find a way to bring her back, don't we? If we just help her do this, aren't we getting off track, helping the dark?"

"No, we're pushing back at the dark because we're doing this to save the kids and to bring back a sister."

"But we didn't save the girl, we let him torture her the take her back. Oh god, she could already be out there with another one ..." Mai fell into Penny's arms again, sobbing her heart out.

Penny held her until she calmed a bit. "Okay, so let's do this different tonight."

"Different, how?"

"We know Kara got the list from a pimp, but she'd already killed him. That john we took out tonight had another girl, and he took her back to a different pimp, so we know there's more. Tonight we save the kid, kill the john, then go deal with the others on the list. After that we go back to the pimp and finish him."

"And save the kids?"

"Absolutely. That's what it's about from now on, save the kids. The priestesses of Moragah are going to do this the right way."

"Penny, thanks for that. I like that idea better. I know you had to make me listen to that tonight so I'd really understand, but that girl paid the price for my education. That hurts.

"But what will we do if we go after one of the johns on the list, and he doesn't have a captive?"

"Honey, these bastards get off on torturing young girls. There's one thing they all have in common, a torture room hidden in their house, a sound proof room where they can listen to the screams but nobody else will know. We go in, find the room, make him confess, then hand him his fate."

"Okay, got it. You get the couch, I get the floor."

"You sure?"

"I'm doing penance. I get the floor."

"Works for me," grinned Penny.

As darkness fell they went back to work. A man arrived home with a girl in his car. He hurried her down to the basement and pushed her into his dungeon. To his horror, there were two women there, dressed in black with blue spirals on their faces.

"Who the fuck are you? How did you get in here? What the hell do you want?"

The smaller girl stepped towards him. "We're her sisters, we broke in, and we want you to call the police and confess everything, tell them about every child you've ever tortured, every minor you've raped."

"And if I don't?"

"I kill you and call them myself. You have ten seconds to decide."

He just stared at her, but didn't move. She struck a single blow and he fell to the floor with a shattered larynx, gagging and trying to get air into his lungs. She stepped over him and took the girl by the hand. "Come on sweetie, let's get you out of here."

"Where are you taking me?" asked the girl as she watched Penny go through his pockets and come up with his car keys.

"I'll drop you off at the police station," said Penny. "You tell them everything and they'll help you get home."

The child burst into tears. "I get to go home?"

"Yes you do, sweetie. It's all over."

Penny drove her to the police station then jumped on the bike with Mai. They were soon at another house. Their target was watching television with a gun in his hand. The door crashed open and they charged inside.

"Oh no you don't," he said as they faced him. His voice trembled in fear. "You're not torturing me." Before Penny could reach him the gun barked and his body fell sideways.

"Chickenshit," muttered Penny as she turned and left the house.

Three more visits and one more rescued girl later they returned for the pimp. They found him in a parking lot near a night club. One moment he was playing a game on his phone and the next he was flying through the air to land heavily against a parked car.

Penny grabbed him by the testicles and jerked him to his feet with a howl of pain. "Where are they?"

"What? Who? ..."

"The girls, where are they?"

"I don't ... ohhh, please ..."

"Tell me or I'll rip them off and feed them to you."

"There." He pointed weakly at a delivery truck parked nearby. "In there. Please ..."

Penny dropped him and stepped to the truck. She tore off the lock and opened the back. There were five frightened girls there. They were all fastened to the wall with collars around their necks and locks securing them.

Mai grabbed the man as he tried to crawl away. She threw him into the truck. "Unlock them. Unlock them or I'll cause you worlds of pain you can't even imagine." Whimpering, he complied.

As the last girl climbed out of the truck, Mai's arm flashed and the man's eyes rolled back trying to see the small throwing knife that had penetrated his skull. His body sank slowly to the floor, twitched a couple of times then lay still.

"Okay, guys, is everybody here or are there more of you out with the johns somewhere?" asked Penny.

"One of us is still out with a master," replied a girl.

"We already got her back," said Penny. "We took her to the police. We'll call them here to help you now."

"Help us?"

"Help you get home, honey. They'll help you get home." She called, told the police she was the Fallen Angel and told them where to find the girls. They waited until the police cars came screaming into the parking lot, then they vanished.

It was late the next afternoon when they found the Chosen in a biker bar. They walked in to a few loud crude and rude cat calls from some of the other people there, but one look from Thunder shut that down.

Kara was completely startled when Mai stepped into her arms and started sobbing. "Oh god, Kara. I'm so sorry I spoke to you the way I did." Wide-eyed, Kara looked over the sobbing girl's shoulder to see a hard-eyed Penny looking back.

Kara rolled her eyes then patted Mai's back. "Aw, come on, girl, don't do this. I can't take it when pretty girls cry." Mai just sniffed and hugged her tighter. Suddenly Kara's hand dropped and she grabbed a handful of girl butt. With a shriek, Mai leaped away from her. "What the hell did you do that for?"

"Do what?" asked Kara, a grin of pure mischief on her face.

"Grab my ass, that's what."

Everybody was laughing at them now. "Well, it's your own damn fault," replied Kara.

"My fault, what do you mean it's my fault?" She took a step back as Kara stepped towards her.

"Well, you're so damn cute and distracting anyway, and then you got all gushy girly on me, I lost my head. I mean, how could I ...?"

"Oh my god, you keep away from me." Mai ducked behind Ryder. "Ryder, make her behave. Stop laughing at me. Kyle, you're supposed to be my boyfriend, why aren't you helping me?"

Laughing, Kyle pulled Mai into a chair beside him. "Come here, sweet cakes, I'll protect you from that horny old Angel." More laughter at Mai's expense.

Blushing and laughing, Mai returned to the table with Kara, Thunder, Ryder and Penny. Kara felt Mai's eyes on her and looked up. "What?"

"Are we okay?"

"Better than," replied Kara, looking at Mai's chest and licking her lips.

"Stop it." Mai folded her arms across her chest and gave Kara a fierce look, but couldn't hold it and burst out laughing. "Gods, you're awful. Kara, I had no real idea, but I got a fast education these past few days. I get it now, and I have no problems at all."

Kara nodded then took a sip of her beer. "So, you guys have been busy. Finish your share of the list?"

"We did," said Penny. "We found a few more in the process. So, are we done here?"

"Done here?"

"With Seattle, are we finished with this town?"

"Far as I know," replied Kara. "You find that cop's niece?"

"Nope. We did look though."

"Yeah, me too. I expect if she's still in this area she'll be in that guy's backyard. If she's alive she'll have been shipped out long ago."

"That's what I figured," sighed Penny. "Where to next?"

"Excuse me?"

Penny leaned forward and looked into Kara's eyes. "I want my sister back, you want revenge on the johns who hurt you, you and far too many others. Fine, I'm good with that. Let's just get it done."

"You're willing to help me? Really?"

"Yes really. Let's do this. I don't give a shit if we have to kill every damned pedophile in the country, let's just do it, but there's no copping out, I want every one of those kids rescued. We take the bastards down, but we save the kids, deal?"

"Deal."

"I'm in," said Mai.

Kara turned those fierce eyes on her. "This is all about motivation for Penny, and I know that. I want some payback for every scream they tore out of my throat. Penny wants to save every kid from that torture, and I have no problem with that. What motivates you?"

"I was forced to sit outside a house and listen to a child scream her lungs out for half the night. I listened to her pray for help, beg for it to stop, and cry for her mother. Penny wouldn't let me help her. We did nothing but wait until we followed him back to the pimp. Only then, when it was too late to answer her sobbing prayers, did we act.

"I got my education, Kara, but somebody else paid for it. Now it's time to put that education to use. From now on I'll be watching for this, and I swear I'll answer every cry for help I hear from a child's throat. You've got a demon inside you and that one's yours to fight, but I plan to fight the rest of them."

Kara smiled gently and nodded. "Accepted. I have no issues, and I accept the help, and, as long as nobody tries to interfere with me, I'm happy to have you along."

"So, where to next?"

Mai's question went unanswered as the bartender approached and whispered to Thunder. He nodded and stood up as the man hurried away. "Merle Downy's been spotted in Portland. Let's ride." Without another word everybody rose and left the bar.

Heading South Again

Thunder was on the phone as they exited the bar. "It's go time, we're on our way south to Portland. We'll head out easy, you guys spread 'em out a bunch." Nobody had a chance to ask what that was all about as the engines began to roar to life.

———◉———

AT POLICE HEADQUARTERS a federal agent snatched up his phone. "They're heading out, moving south."

"Portland or Olympia," he said, as he stuffed the phone back into his pocket. "Let's go." He led the way and soon he was in a helicopter speeding towards the highway south. "Let them get out onto the open highway. We don't want anything to go crazy while they're still in the city."

A while later they reached the open road and another helicopter made contact with them. "Which group are we following again?"

"What do you mean, which group?"

"Sir, there's at least a dozen groups of riders on the highway south. Which group is the target?"

"What? It's the Chosen. They wear a huge blue spiral on their back with Chosen written above it. There are about thirty riders in the group."

"Understood. Repeat, which group of the Chosen?"

"I just told you."

"Sir, from here I count seven groups of about thirty riders. All groups have multiple riders in Chosen colors."

"Oh for fuck sake. Those dirty bastards. Look for a small female rider, blond hair."

"Understood."

A few more minutes and he was flying over the highway. There had to be hundreds of motorcycles on the road. The other chopper contacted him again. "Sir, there's at least two or more small female riders in each group. Please advise."

Before the agent could respond the other chopper sounded the alarm. "She's running."

"Report. What's happening?"

"Small female rider just broke from the group below us. She passing the next group and still accelerating."

"Get after her. Mark that target, do not lose sight of that rider."

A few moments later the voice returned. "We still have eyes on the rider, Sir. She's been absorbed into another group and the following group has melded with it. Sir, the road blocks are in place."

"Isolate that group and stop them. Get the rest of the bikers off the road as quickly as possible. We don't want this to get out of hand."

"Roger that."

———— ◉ ————

DOWN ON THE HIGHWAY things were getting interesting. A chopper flew past, then a half dozen police cars and a SWAT van blew past. Thunder grinned as he held the speed of his group back. Further on they came to a roadblock. There were over twenty police vehicles plus three helicopters surrounding a group of about fifty riders.

The riders were milling about while the police fought to gain control and identify each of them. They were also trying to separate out the smaller female riders.

As they reached the scene the police waved them on through. "Move it, move along, nothing to see here. Move along." Thunder grinned as they drove past the blockade.

Once the highway was clear of motorcycles the federal agent began sorting out the mess. Men and taller women were quickly sent away.

Finally only a few shorter men and a half dozen women remained. "All right, get those helmets off, now."

Slowly they complied. Everyone was grinning. When the helmets were on the ground and the women's faces exposed, the agent started to swear profusely. They had three Hispanic girls, one black woman of about forty, an Asian, and a well tanned brunette with deep brown eyes.

Finally, he stopped swearing and spoke. "All you people are under arrest."

"What for?" asked the black woman.

"We'll start with aiding and abetting a known felon."

"I don't think so," she replied. She passed him her ID. Margaret S. Browne, attorney at law. "Oh you can take us in if you want, but it'll only get worse. To start with, while you're proving how tough and in control you are, the one you're after will have even more time to elude you."

"Dammit, woman, do you know who's riding with the Chosen?"

"Well, there's about ninety-seven of us at last count. I don't know everybody personally ..."

"That's not what I mean and you know it. The Fallen Angel is riding with the Chosen and we know they were in Seattle heading south. You people deliberately aided in her escape."

"I don't know anything about the vigilante who calls herself the Fallen Angel. If she truly was in one of the other groups, then you waved her on yourselves. She'll be in Olympia by now."

"All right, if you're all so innocent, tell me why so many of you were on the road today?"

"We got word of a joint ride with several other groups. Somebody called in big favors, and we were told we were looking for a child of about twelve to fourteen named Grace. They said we might find her on the road to Portland.

"Our groups were just supposed to ride down as far as Olympia and see what we could find out. Other groups left Olympia heading south, and so on. That's all we're doing, looking for a lost child. If you know the Chosen, you know we do that a lot."

"Yeah, right. Ah fuck it, we blew that one. Let them go, they're just stalling us anyway."

———————⬤———————

ON A HILLSIDE OUTSIDE of Olympia Washington, a group of riders set up camp for the night. "That was pretty slick, Thunder," said Kara as she settled down by the small fire.

"Yeah, it was sweet all right," he replied, passing her a beer.

"The best part was when that cop waved us through and told us to move our asses, we were blocking traffic."

"Yeah. I loved that part."

"So, what exactly happened? Why did they wave us through?"

"We figured they'd be up to something. You guys really cleaned house in Seattle. No way that was going to pass unchallenged. I made a few calls and set it up. As soon as we were on the road, another rider about your size made a run for it. She zipped ahead until she had the choppers on her tail then faded into another group.

"Once she was tucked in, the other groups started bunching up around her. The cops went for it and waved the rest of us on through to keep the bunch up from getting bigger."

"Yeah, but they had her marked, right. What'll they do to her?"

"Not a damn thing, Angel. Maggie's a kick ass lawyer with a mean reputation. She'll be fine."

"There's a lawyer in the Chosen?"

"Yup, we pulled her youngest out of a bad situation a couple of years ago. Maggie bought a bike and signed on. Woman's tough as nails."

"Wow."

Penny and Mai joined them. "So, not going hunting tonight?"

"Nope. I have no issues with this town. You guys?"

"I've got nothing," replied Penny. "Mai?"

"No, I'm good."

"I've got an errand in town," said Kyle.

"She ready, Kyle?" asked Thunder. Kyle nodded. "Okay, let's you and me head into town for a beer."

"What's going on?" asked Penny.

Kara grinned. "I'd say a few pimps are about to buy Ryder her own bike. The boys will be taking up a collection. About damn time too."

"Pretty proud of her, aren't you? She remind you of somebody?"

"Yeah, I am proud of her, Penny. The girl's got grit. I was totally messed up until Moragah got me straightened out a bit, but Ryder seems to be handling it way better. Ryder's tougher than I was."

Her voice sounded wistful and Penny smiled.

"She had a harder start," said Mai. "You had a loving family and a normal childhood until you were taken, Ryder didn't. She'd already been through hell before she was slaved out."

"You could be right about that," sighed Kara. She crushed the beer can in her hand and tossed it away.

Mai rose and retrieved it, putting it in a plastic bag she carried in her backpack. "Litterbug," she accused.

"Hey, I'm the bad guy, we do bad things like that," grumbled Kara. Mai giggled and so did Penny. Kara laughed then shook her head. "You guys are nuts."

"You like us," said Penny.

"Yes I do, my sisters, yes I do."

Portland

Next day they set out early, stopping once to buy a used bike for Ryder, then continuing on their way to Portland. The Chosen got visible and Penny led Mai and Kara to the place where she had busted up the Portland operation there years prior. Damned if it wasn't back in operation.

"Let me tell you how this one works," said Penny.

"I already know how it works," replied Kara, a snarl on her lips and bloody murder in her eyes.

"Easy, girl, easy, we want to get the kids out, all of them."

With a visible effort Kara reined in the rage that threatened to overwhelm her. "Okay, but no pimp or john survives to start up again, that's the deal."

"Agreed," sighed Penny. "Last time I was here we had the bloodline helping. They followed the johns and kept in touch by cell phone. We caught up, saved the girl, then dropped her off someplace safe. This time will be different."

"Tell me," said a hard eyed Kara.

"This time I follow the john, put him down, then drop the girl off with the cops. Mai, I'm walking a fine line here, and if you want to pass this by, I'll understand."

"Take a pass? No way I'm taking a pass on this one. Our job is to defend the weak, so that's what I'm planning to do, save the girl and finish the john. By doing that, I will be saving a lot of innocent girls from torture at his hands in the future. I'm in."

"We're looking for a kid named Grace and a man named Merle Downy, too. Don't forget that," said Penny.

"I'm not likely to forget that," said Kara, as she slipped over the edge of the roof and set out after a car that had just picked up a girl.

"Penny, tell me the truth now, are we slipping over to the darkness? Aren't we supposed to be the good guys? Do the good guys just kill the bad guys?

"Maybe we should ask Moragah about this?"

"Works for me. Lady Moragah?"

"I am here, my daughters. I sense your distress. Listen carefully to me now. You are only doing what must be done. There is no other way to stop these men, no other way to prevent them from repeating what they do. Many of the men Kara has killed are ones Penny stopped once before.

"Know this, my children, death is not the end of the spirit's journey, merely another step along the path. It is a sadness that it has come to this, but these men have completely embraced the darkness, there is no pity or compassion in them."

"Nor Kara either," said Mai.

"No, Mai, Kara still has compassion for the victims, but only them. It grieves me you both have had to move closer to the dark to reach her, but reach her you have. I can sense the dark's grip on her loosening. We still have a long way to go, but I believe we will succeed."

"If we don't fall into the darkness first."

"You must be wary, my priestesses. The darkness you face now is the worst form of evil. Ever it will try to draw you in, to break your spirit. You felt this, both of you, the night Penny held you back so you would know fully and understand what Kara has experienced.

"Be wary, my daughters, but do what you must. Just keep in mind the young women you are saving and those who will never know such torment because you prevented it from happening. Proceed, my priestesses, and know I am with you always. I will be ever present in this quest. Please tell Kara I'm always trying to reach her."

They had no more time as another car was leaving the alley. "Mine," snarled Mai as she dropped from the roof top and mounted her bike.

"Oh sure," muttered Penny, "take the damn bike. Leave the oldest sister to follow a guy on foot. Bugger that."

She slipped over the eave and dropped to the ground. She'd just seen a pick up truck coming out of the alley. The driver was completely unaware as a shadow hopped into the bed of the truck and rode along as he drove his victim home to his torture chamber.

———◉———

TERRIFIED, YET UTTERLY resigned to her fate, the girl obeyed the order to strip off her clothes and lie face down on the table. Her ankles and wrists were fastened tightly then the whip sang. The blow didn't land. She heard a gasp and then a cry of pain behind her, and then a voice filled with command.

"Release her," commanded that voice from a distant hell. Trembling in fear, the man obeyed.

Once she was free a gentle voice spoke to her. "Hey girl, what's your name?"

"Melody."

"Cool, pretty name. Okay, Melody, you get dressed, then we'll deal with this asshole." Wide-eyed and terrified, the girl obeyed the small figure wearing the faceless mask.

"Please don't kill me," begged the man.

"Oh no, buddy boy, that's not on the table. We are definitely going to kill you. The only question is, how much pain will you endure before we do the deed. Get your clothes off and get on that table."

Whimpering and weeping, he obeyed her. He tried begging again as she tightened the straps that bound his wrists and ankles. She ignored him and turned to the girl. "He ever had you on that table before?"

"Yes."

"How many times?"

"Seven."

"Okay, here's his whip. Give him a taste of his own medicine." With a grin of delight the girl snatched the whip from her hand and used it with gusto. Kara let her go until her arms hung at her side from fatigue. The man was weeping and sobbing, begging for mercy.

"You know something, girl, I've noticed that these assholes can dish it out, but they just can't take it, not like you and me."

"You too?" asked the girl, wide-eyed.

"Yeah, me too. Now, I need your help with some stuff, you up for it?"

"Uh, yeah, I guess."

"It'll be fun. First, though, tell me if any of the other girls where they keep you are named Grace." The child shook her head. "Ah well, it was worth a shot. Okay, here's the fun part. I'm gonna ask this dipshit some questions. If he lies to me or doesn't answer, you whip his ass until he does, okay?"

The girl nodded fiercely then gripped the whip with both hands. She nodded that she was ready. Kara stepped out where the man could see her then took off the mask. "Remember me?"

His jaw went slack as he recognized her, but he made no sound. She nodded at the child who swung the whip with all her strength. He screamed and his body jerked violently as the leather strip bit into his already tormented flesh. "Yes, yes," he howled.

"That's 'yes, Mistress,'" said the girl, as she swung the whip again. "Let me hear you say it." Crack! "Call her Mistress, or I'll beat you to death with this frigging whip." The whip connected again. Kara just grinned.

"Yes, Mistress. Yes I remember you, Mistress."

"Very good, so, next question, do you know who I am now?"

"Yes, Mistress, yes. You're the Fallen Angel now, Mistress."

"Good boy. Now let's get to the good stuff. Do you know a man named Merle Downy?"

His eyes told the truth of it even before his lips spoke the words. "Yes, Mistress."

"Tell me where he is."

"I don't know, Mistress." Kara nodded and the whip sang. "No, Mistress, I don't know. I'm telling the truth. I don't know where he is. He left two days ago, Mistress."

"Tell me where he went."

"Please, Mistress, I don't know where he is. He's out hunting, somewhere."

"Hunting? Explain."

The man was sobbing now, completely broken. "He's broke, Mistress. He needs money."

"So, he's out there hunting for girls."

"Yes, Mistress."

"That dirty fucking bastard. I know how he works. If he catches a girl he'll want to train her himself, so he'll need a place to work. Where would he take her?"

"I don't know." Kara nodded and he screamed even before the lash struck his flesh. She laughed cruelly and nodded again. "Mistress, please, I don't know. He'll go to Albert's place, but I don't know where it is, nobody does. Somewhere in California."

"Tell me about Albert. Who is he? What's his claim to fame?"

"Albert's an unknown," sobbed the man. "He comes online once in a while with great pictures, but he doesn't talk to anybody unless they will bring him a present."

"Keep going, what kind of a present?"

"Please, Mistress ..."

Again Kara nodded and the whip whistled through the air. When the screaming stopped he sobbed out the story. "Albert's pictures were of him killing the victim. To visit his place a gift of a girl to torture and kill has to be presented.

"He's been known to allow Merle Downey to train a girl at his place before, but only if he brought two, one to train for sale and one for Albert to play with.

"Others have gone there too, but Albert always meets them in the city, and they're taken to his place blindfolded. Merle's the only person Albert ever trusted with the location of his farm."

"So, Albert's death camp, his farm, is about two hours out of LA. Have you ever been there?"

He denied it, but his eyes gave him away. She nodded and then waited until he stopped screaming. "Well, that seals it. Come on, Melody, let's get out of here."

"Aren't we going to kill him? You said we would."

"Yes, my sister, we'll set the place on fire and let him burn with it. Let's go." They hurried up the stairs, ignoring the man's pleas for mercy. When they reached the top Kara sent a lance of hellfire back into the basement. He was still screaming as they rode away on her motorcycle.

Kara dropped the girl off at the police station then returned to the roof top where she found both Penny and Mai waiting. She related what she'd learned and Mai lost her last meal.

"I didn't believe this could get any worse," Mai said weakly, "but it just did."

"Yeah," said Kara, "this is some seriously sick shit."

Penny nodded, also fighting to keep her stomach from heaving up. "So, are we going after Merle?"

"Not yet," replied Kara. "We've still got a lot of work to do here." The others nodded their agreement. "It's getting late now; the other johns will soon be bringing the kids back."

"Do we follow them to their homes and take them out?" asked Mai.

"Yup, indeed we do," replied Kara. "So, Penny, did I see a pickup truck down there?"

"Yeah, well, Mai took off with the bike so I had to hitch a ride with the john. He doesn't have any use for it anymore so I borrowed it for a while. Cops will blame you for it anyway."

Kara chuckled at that. "Oops, looks like we have incoming."

"Hey, you want to take this operation down?"

"Not right now, Mai," replied Kara. "We've got a few more johns to finish first. How about we deal with this lot, then come back here and take this bunch apart?"

"I'm in," said Penny. "Let's do it." She hopped down from the roof then they heard the truck start.

Two hours later the sun was coming up. They'd reassembled at the rooftop. "So, how do we do this?" asked Mai.

"It's tough to bust," replied Kara. "If it wasn't for the kids I'd burn the fuckers out. How did you do it last time, Penny."

"We used a john returning, with Tara pretending to be the girl. So, here's what we do. You've got issues here, Kara, so I'll pretend to be dropping you off. Once you're inside you can do your thing. Just send those kids out to me and I'll get them to safety."

"Won't work, you need a pass code and they change it every day. The john calls for a girl and they give him the pass code for when he returns her."

"Not a problem, the dumbass I took out wrote it down and left it in the truck."

"Sweet," grinned Kara. "We're in business. Let's go."

"Hey you guys, what's my role here?" asked Mai.

"You help me get the kids into the truck," replied Penny, "then follow me on the bike. As soon as we drop them off I'll abandon the truck and you pick me up. We all meet back at the campsite."

"Gotcha, let's go."

They dropped down from the roof and got in the truck. It worked like a charm. Penny sat in the truck grinning as she heard gunfire and screams from inside. Soon enough the door opened and five girls came out. They snuggled them in with Penny and she drove to the police station.

Penny watched until the girls disappeared through the door then she drove away. She abandoned the truck in a mall parking lot then hopped on the bike with Mai.

They were just settling in for a rest when they heard Kara's bike returning. "I take it we're not in a hurry today," said Thunder, as he yawned and stretched.

"Nope, nor tomorrow neither," replied Kara.

"Kara?"

"I found out those guys have some competition, Penny, there's another kiddy pimp operating in town. I thought I'd look him up after about ten hours sleep."

"Works for me, sis," sighed Penny, as she settled down under a tree.

Kara just snorted and shook her head. "That girl can sleep anywhere. You guys got any beer?"

"Get some rest, Angel," grinned Thunder. "We'll pick some up for you this afternoon."

"Deal," she said, as she stretched out near Penny and went to sleep.

Finishing Up and Moving On

Darkness was falling as Kara awoke from tormented dreams. Sweat rolled down from her brow and her eyes were wild as she sat up with a start. "Sweet baby Jesus," she sighed, as she tried to shake off the dream. "Did I hurt anybody?"

"No, but you got the campfire going again nicely," grinned Kyle.

"Dammit, Kyle, one of these days ..." She didn't finish the threat, but jogged off to the facilities instead. She returned looking more awake, but still rattled. "So, did you guys pick up that beer?"

"They did," said Ryder, "but I got you something to eat. You eat first then you get beer."

Kara accepted the sub sandwich and took a bite. "So, when did you become my mom?"

"The day you brought my sorry ass out of slavery. I never had a big sister before and want you to last. Have some water with that." She passed over a bottle of water.

"Thanks, this is a bit dry. Where did the gruesome twosome go?"

"Penny and Mai?"

"Yeah, them."

"Penny said she was going undercover as a street person to see if she can find where the kids are being held. Man, Kara, you weren't kidding when you said you could take out a city block. We saw what was left of the place after the firemen got the fire out late this morning."

"Yeah," said Thunder as he joined them. "They said it was burning too hot to fight so they let it go and tried to save the surrounding buildings. They're sifting through the ashes for any signs of a body in there. They gonna find any?"

"Several. Bastards. Okay, Mom, I finished my breakfast and drank my water. Can I have my medication now?" Ryder laughed and passed her a beer. "Nectar of the gods," She said as she popped open the can and took a sip.

"Getting in the mood again?" asked Ryder.

"Yup, there's still more work to do here before we head back to California."

"You were hollering a lot in your sleep, Angel," said Thunder. "You were threatening to kill somebody named Albert. Aren't we after Merle?"

"Sorry about that, guys," sighed Kara. She drained the can of beer then wiped her mouth on her sleeve. "Okay, here's the story on Albert. It seems he's an old buddy of Merle's. He lives on a farm somewhere about two hours out of LA. They have a secret death camp set up there."

"Death camp?"

"Yeah, death camp, Ryder. They take the girls there, torture them to death then put up pictures on the internet. Old Albert is one crafty and careful bastard. Apparently Merle's the only one who knows where the place is. Others have been there, but he meets them in the city and takes them out there blindfolded.

"To get an invitation to the farm they have to bring Albert a present, a girl to torture and kill. It can't be one like us either, she has to be untouched."

"Virgin?"

"No, Thunder, just never tortured before."

"So why the fuck aren't we going after this piece of shit?"

"We are. Count on it, we're definitely going after him, him and Merle. Merle's been there before, several times as I understand it. Trust me, those fuckers are going straight to hell the hard way. The trick is, to find them."

"You want the Chosen to ask around a bit?"

"Yup. As soon as we finish up here, you guys head for LA and see what you can find out."

"Aren't you coming with us?" asked Ryder.

"No, sis, not at first. Here's the plan. Tonight, with Penny and Mai to help, we should be able to finish up here. If we get lucky and find a lead to Albert's farm tonight, then we all head south together. I doubt we'll get that lucky. It's never that easy finding these bastards.

"So, if we come up empty, I'll be back tracking a bit to a cop I met recently. He's one of the guys who works on this shit, you know, undercover on the internet. He might have something and not know it. I'll talk to him then head straight for LA and meet up with you guys.

"Relax, I'm not trying to run out on you guys again. I need you. Hell, I'm under age, I need you guys to buy beer for me."

"Now there was a hint if I ever heard one," chuckled Kyle, as he tossed her another can from the cooler. A few moments later Penny and Mai returned.

"You guys have any luck locating the kids?" asked Kara.

Penny sighed as she sank down beside her. "Yeah, we found them. It's a bit early yet. Give me time to get some food into me then we'll go get set up." Kara nodded her approval.

"Okay, we're saving the kids, eliminating the johns and the pimp, and looking for Grace, right?" said Mai. "Tell me we're also trying to get a location for that death camp."

"Oh yeah, that we are," replied Kara. "I'm going to find it, kill both those bastards, then burn that fucking place down with fire so hot Satan himself would turn on the air conditioner."

"Please don't burn it, Kara."

"Penny?"

"Look, I agree with how you feel here, I do, but the gods alone know how many girls are buried on that damn farm. If we let the cops have the place they can use DNA testing to identify some of them, bring closure to some families anyway."

"I guess," Kara replied sourly.

"Look, I'll find you a nice pimp's hideout to burn down, okay?"

Kara laughed at that. "Okay, as long as you promise I get to play."

IT WAS A POORER AREA of town with a lot of unsavory nightlife in evidence. Hookers walked the streets openly, drugs and money changed hands frequently, and worse. Three sets of hard eyes watched from an alleyway as a car pulled up, money changed hands, and a girl got out of the van and into the car.

As the car pulled away a darkened motorcycle followed at a distance. This wasn't like the standard sex trade. There'd be no stop in an alley and a quick romp for a few dollars. These girls were expensive, and the johns needed a place with equipment to get what they desperately wanted.

It had to be a place that was unseen as well as sound proof. Fortunately for them, the habit of building panic rooms into houses worked in their favor. A few had even managed to buy older houses with bomb shelters still functional.

The girl sat quietly as he drove along, heading out of town and into the suburbs. He sang along off key to the music blaring from the music system, his voice trembling slightly in his excitement.

He'd been saving up for months to afford this night. This was it, he planned to take lots of pictures to upload for the network. At no point in time did he notice the dark rider following him like the angel of death. Oh yes, there would be screams this night all right.

It was only when he pulled into the driveway that he checked his mirrors carefully, but all looked quiet. He hit the remote and the garage door opened. It slid closed behind the car once it was inside.

She was already on the property, sitting quietly, listening with all her enhanced hearing, waiting for the sound of the torture room door closing. As soon as he ordered the girl to strip, she moved. A door was forced, and she was inside.

"Get your bare ass over in front of that camera. Don't even dream of that freak, the Fallen Angel coming to rescue you and kill me. The cops are all over this town tonight and she'll be long gone by now."

"No she won't," came a soft voice from behind him.

He spun around and raised the whip, but she just laughed at him. "Seriously? The whip? Is that what you've got? Oh man, are you in trouble. Girl, put your clothes back on. Nobody's going to hurt you tonight."

The man stood trembling in fear, still clutching his whip while the girl got dressed. The angel didn't move. Once the girl was dressed Kara told her to move behind her. "Okay, buddy, are you ready?"

He was shaking so badly now he actually dropped the whip. She laughed at him. "You know who I am, but do you know how I do it, do you? No? All right, I'll tell you. First I bust into the pedophile's place and confront him. That's where we are now.

"Okay, next I make him strip then tie him down and let the girl whip his ass until he screams like a little baby. That's when I start asking questions. If he tells me the truth, it's all good and I kill him quick.

"If he lies to me the girl gets to use the whip again until he gets around to telling the truth. Then I kill him slow. That's how I work." The man swallowed hard and wet himself.

She smiled cruelly and took a step towards him. He began to whimper and backed away. "You're actually a lucky fella, you know why?" Unable to find his voice, he just shook his head. "It's because I don't know you, and you never had me in this shit hole. The guys I killed? They all had me at one time or another. That's what this is all about, payback.

"So, now we get to the point of my visit here tonight. I'm looking for a few things. If you play fair with me I have no reason to kill you. Deal?" He nodded his head eagerly.

"Girl, you still there?"

"Yes."

"Is your name Grace?"

"No."

"Too bad. What is it?"

"Irene."

"Okay, Irene. Has this guy ever had you here before?"

"Yes, twice."

"What's his favorite deal? What does he like to do to you the most?"

"He makes me take off my clothes and kneel. Then he ..."

"Okay, I get that part. What about the rest of this stuff?"

"He ties me over that bench with my wrists tied to my ankles then he hits me with that bamboo stick on the back of my legs. It really hurts."

"Yes it does, my sister. Yes it does. Okay buddy, this girl is now Mistress Irene. Get your clothes off and bend over that bench."

"No, please ..."

"Do it willingly or I'll do it for you. Believe me, it'll hurt a hell of a lot more if Mistress Angel does the interrogation." Whimpering in fear he complied.

Once Kara had secured him she grinned and passed the cane to the girl. "Give him a taste of his own medicine, you know, just to get him in the right mood."

Swinging the thin cane like a baseball bat the child struck the backs of his legs. His body jerked violently and he screamed. Kara let her hit him a few more times then stopped her. "Okay, buddy, Mistress Irene wants to know if you've ever had a girl named Grace in here."

"I don't know, I don't know. I don't want to know their names."

"You forgot to say Mistress Irene. That's two lashes with the whip." She tossed the whip to the girl, and although he begged and pleaded as well as shouted 'Mistress Irene' several times, she still used the whip with gusto.

Again Kara stopped her. The cruel smile was still on her lips as she pulled his head up by the hair and looked into his terrified eyes. "Not nearly so much fun from this side, is it asshole? So, now Mistress Irene wants to know if you've ever looked at pictures of girls being tortured on the internet?"

"Yes, Mistress Irene," he sobbed.

"Good boy. Now Mistress Irene wants to know if you have ever seen pictures put up by a man named Albert."

His eyes gave him away and he knew it. "Yes, Mistress Irene."

"Now she wants to know where he is."

"I don't know, I swear I don't know."

"You forgot to say Mistress Irene again."

He howled out the name mixed with his screams of pain as the child whipped the backs of his stretched hamstrings. "Okay, don't forget her name again, it makes her angry. Now, back to Albert, did you ever save any of his pictures on your computer?"

He was weeping now. "Yes, Mistress Irene."

"Are they still there?"

"Yes, Mistress Irene."

"All right, now Mistress Irene wants you to print off a few of those pictures. I'm going to let you loose, and you're going to behave yourself if you want to stay alive. You'll take us to the computer, find those pictures for me, and I'll tell which ones to print."

"Can I put the collar on him?" asked Irene.

"The collar?"

"It's a pinch collar for a dog. He makes me wear it because he says I'm as ugly as a dog's ass."

"Oh yes, my sister, put the collar on him then I'll let him loose."

She found the collar and leash. As soon as it was on him she gave it a hard jerk. "Heel." Kara laughed as she unhooked the wrist and ankle cuffs.

The child made him crawl up the stairs to the computer. Trembling in fear, he opened the file. Kara fought to keep her stomach down. The pictures showed a girl being tortured then her throat was cut and she was butchered like a hog, her body hung on meat hooks with the bodies of the pigs, then skinned out.

"Don't look," she said as she put out an arm to stop the girl. "You don't need to see this, my sister." She waited while the pictures were printed off.

With a sudden burst of rage she grabbed the hapless pedophile and snapped his neck. "I swear I'll kill every fucking one of you sick and twisted bastards." She folded the prints and tucked them into her jacket.

"Come on, Irene. I'll drop you off with the police. They'll help you get home."

"You really mean it? I get to go home?"

The girl burst into tears and Kara held her until the storm of emotion passed. "Yeah, you get to go home now, honey. It's all over. Let's go."

Kara dropped her off at the police station and watched until she disappeared through the door. As soon as Irene told her story the police went looking. They eventually found the dead man with the pictures still up on his computer. Both officers vomited at the sight on the screen.

So did Penny and Mai when she showed them the pictures.

Backtracking

"So, we're headed back to LA and you're going somewhere else?" asked Penny.

"I'll catch up in a few days, I promise."

"Kara ..."

"Penny, I'm not trying to run out on you, I swear it. You know how bad I want these guys."

"I was trying to say, be careful."

Kara gave a sheepish grin. "Sorry, a bit paranoid over here. Mai, will you take my bike to LA for me?"

"Sure, love to."

"Don't scratch the paint."

"I wouldn't think of it."

"Ah-huh. Ryder, can you give me a lift into town."

"Sure, but ..."

"Look, guys, the cops are looking for a small blond on a bike, I need to steal a car and do some backtracking. I met this cop outside Denver. He's one of those under cover internet guys, trying to catch pedophiles. He might actually have something on Albert.

"I'll return to LA same way we got here. Don't worry, I'll find you."

"Kara ..."

"No, Penny, I won't leave you out of this one. If I find anything we'll go in together. The only rule here is Merle and Albert die, Merle by my hand. You ride in with the Chosen, I'll find you guys, I promise."

If anyone had been watching, they would have seen five riders and one passenger ride into town and stop at a bar. Three hours later five riders left and returned to the campsite. Once darkness fell, a shadow watched the patrons arriving at a night club.

When she saw the one she wanted she dropped down from the rooftop then moved into the throng of people. After bumping into a few people she made her way to the parking lot. The keys to the car were in the purse she'd lifted from the tipsy woman who'd staggered slightly as she headed for the club.

While the woman partied on, her car headed out for Denver with a different blond behind the wheel. Kara stopped to do some shopping in Salt Lake City then rented a motel room for the night.

The next morning a different looking girl left Salt Lake City for Denver. Gone was the biker babe look. She now looked more like a glamor girl. Kara swapped out the license plates with another car and continued on her journey.

Her plan was simple, find Albert. Once she had a location for him she had Merle. The key now was to find Albert and for that she would need allies, not just the Chosen, but allies in law enforcement.

Arlo unlocked the door and stepped aside to let his wife enter first. He frowned as he heard Keisha giggle in the kitchen. "No, silly, not like that, this way."

"Dammit, she knows better than to bring friends home when we're not here," he said, as he brushed past his wife and headed towards the sounds of laughter.

"Keisha, you know the rules. Keep the doors locked and no friends in until ..." he stopped speaking as he saw who was there.

"It's okay, Daddy, it's Angel. I'm trying to teach her how to play the last video game you got me, but she's not very good at it."

"Hey you." The girl giggled again and leaned away from Kara who made a face and stuck out her tongue at her. That made the girl laugh harder.

Arlo swallowed hard. It took a moment for him to find his voice. "Why are you here?"

"I need your help to find somebody."

"Don't do this to me, please. Don't make me an accessory to murder again."

She picked up a large brown envelope and tossed it to him. "Look in there."

"Please, I ..."

"Just look in there. After that if you still don't want to help me I'll go."

He sighed as he picked it up. "Girl, I swear I've seen it all a dozen times since I got this assignment."

"Just look at it," she said, her voice soft, almost pleading.

"Fine, I'll look." He opened the envelope and glanced down, then pulled out the pictures and began to look through them, his wife looking over his shoulder. As it sank in what they were seeing the woman ran for the sink and lost her last meal. He was soon beside her.

"No, Keisha, no," said Kara as she caught the girl's arm to prevent her from going to look at the pictures. "Honey, you don't need to see those pictures, trust me. You don't even want to."

"What are they?"

"Pictures of what bad people do to girls like us."

"Like the people you kill?"

"Yeah, that kind of people. I need your dad to help me locate one special man if he can. I really want to find this guy."

"Are you going to kill him if you find him?"

"Yes I am."

"It's wrong to kill people."

"Yes, you're right, it is wrong to hurt people. Sometimes the world is a nasty place and sometimes I do things I shouldn't so your dad won't have to."

His face ashen, Arlo found his voice. "Are those real?"

"Yes, they are. I need to find this man. Stop playing the game and help me."

"My god, my dear god." His hands trembled as he gripped the back of the chair then sat down. Kara scooped up the pictures, tucked them back inside her jacket, then took Jean by the arm and helped her to the table as well.

"Look, I don't know what you expect me to do here?"

"I know how you make a living, what your job is. I need to know if you've ever heard of this death camp before. Keisha honey, maybe you shouldn't listen to this."

"No, Mom, Angel says I need to know stuff, to be aware of what goes on ..."

It was Kara who stopped her. "Not this time, sweetie. Some stuff is just too bad to express."

"No, I want to know."

"Okay, maybe you're right. This is about a bad man, a man who is far worse than any I have ever encountered before. His name is Albert. He has a farm a few hours outside of LA, California. On his farm he has a secret place where he tortures, then kills, girls like us. He's a nasty piece of work and I need to find him."

The girl was silent, absorbing what she'd been told. "Dad has been teaching me how to be watchful, not just for me, but for everybody. He's teaching me to shoot too, and I know where the guns are kept.

"They can still get me, can't they?"

"They can always try," replied Kara, "but you're smart, way smarter than me, so you watch for them and don't let them get you.

"Now, about Albert. He's well known in certain circles on the internet. However, he's a mystery, rarely comes on, but the sickos all get lit up when he does because he posts this kind of thing.

"Nobody knows where he lives. You can visit him, but you have to bring him a girl child to kill. He meets you in the city and takes you to the farm blindfold. Only one man I am aware of knows how to find the place on his own. Merle Downy."

"Merle Downy, he's the one you were looking for the last time you were here."

"That's right. Here's the thing. I've been on Merle's trail for months now and he keeps slipping through my fingers. However, that's cost him his last cent and every friend he ever had. Merle's run out of options. He has to go to Albert, and he has to capture two girls before he does."

"Why two girls?" asked Jean.

"One for Albert to kill and one to train for a life like I had. He's broke, he needs to sell a girl to get enough money to stay on the run."

"Oh my god," breathed Jean. "Arlo ..."

"Dammit all to hell, you're right, Angel. The official line is way too slow. We get a few but they just seem to keep coming. Fuck it, I'll do whatever I can. Tell me what you need."

"We know they're in California, somewhere. You're constantly on the net, checking on these guys, worming your way into their confidence. Anything you can do to get me closer to these scum, any hint or lead I might follow. Anything at all.

"Arlo, don't even think about setting me up."

"No, trust me, that's not going to happen, Angel." He pushed the envelope of pictures back across the table towards her. "If I set you up, help put you in prison, I might get a raise, a medal, maybe even a better assignment, but how many more girls like Keisha would end up in that monster's hands?

"No girl, this has gone too far, this is ..." Tears of frustration filled his eyes, and his voice failed him.

Kara reached out to grip his arm tightly, startling him with her strength. "Keep it together now, my friend. I promise you; I will make this stop; I just need to find them. The butcher's name is Albert, and the slaver is Merle Downy. Have you got anything on them at all?"

He took a shuddering breath to regain control of his emotions. "Not right off the top of my head. Let me check my computer."

"I checked it, nothing there."

"You checked it? How did you ...?"

"Keishajean? Seriously? That was the best password you could come up with?"

"Fine, Miss Critic, what would you suggest?"

"Spell it backwards," she grinned.

"So, how do I contact you?"

"I've got the home phone number. I'll check in from time to time. You keep these pictures, just to remind yourself of why you're helping me, I've got more. I'll be on my way now; I'll call in a day or two."

As she stood up to leave he suddenly looked puzzled. "What?"

"A miniskirt and heels? Isn't that a bit awkward on a motorcycle?"

"A motorcycle, what makes you think I ride a motorcycle?"

"It's well known you ride with that bike gang, the Chosen."

"Seriously? Now how do you suppose a rumor like that got started?" She smiled and went to the door. "Be good to yourselves, people." With that she was out the door and gone. They heard a car start on the street then they were alone.

Arlo sighed again. "Keisha, honey, you know you're not supposed to let anybody ..."

"I didn't, Daddy, she was already here when I got home. She said she came in through your bedroom window and that you should always remember to lock it."

"Yeah, I guess."

"Arlo, what is it?"

"How did this all happen, Jeannie? What have I become? What will happen to the both of you if anyone ever finds out I helped the Fallen Angel?"

"Then nobody should ever find out."

"So what happens if she keeps coming back for more information about more people?"

"Then we give it to her," replied Jean, a hard look in her eye.

"Yeah, you're right," he said, as he pushed the envelope with his finger. "The system is failing miserably trying to stop these people, but she's proving to be effective. You're right, we help her all we can, and pray she stays free to get it done. I just hope she finds this bastard soon."

———————◉———————

WHILE KARA WAS TALKING with Arlo, the Chosen were camped outside San Francisco. Penny sat brooding as she gazed into the campfire. "I can hear the wheels turning from here," said Thunder. "What's got you bugged, Blue?"

"I'm thinking we might be missing an opportunity here."

"Oh? You thinking we should have a look around Frisco to see if we can scare up some information for Angel?"

"Yup, I am. We know this shit goes on everywhere and here we are in a city where we could do some good."

"So, what's the problem?"

"The problem, my friend, is we don't want to tip this Albert off, send him on the run to start up someplace else."

"Yeah, Angel wouldn't like that. She made it plain she was after Merle's hide and somebody tipped him off. She's been on his trail ever since."

"Yes, and we both know that she knows who it was who put him wise."

"She knows, but hasn't done anything about it."

"Yet."

"Yet?"

"I have a good idea who it was, and I'm praying Kara doesn't go after her. Kara was lured into Merle's car by a friend who was already one of his victims. This woman isn't a predator, she's a fellow victim. If Kara hurts her I'll never be able to get her back."

"Relax, Blue. Angel told me about that. She already confronted the woman, but didn't hurt her."

"She did?"

"Yep, she gambled they wouldn't warn him, but they must have. She's not pissed about it. She knows she'll catch Merle sooner or later. The other woman's suffered enough already."

Penny sighed and sat back against a tree. "Wow, so she's not going to go after that woman?"

"Nope. Now, how about we all saddle up and go see what kind of trouble we can stir up."

"Good plan, let's do it."

Mai grinned as Penny rose to her feet. "Well it's about time, I thought I was going to be hunting on my own tonight."

"Not a chance, sweet sister. We'll let the boys beat up a few pimps while we see if we can locate some people up to bad things." Mai laughed as she leaped aboard the motorcycle and fired it up.

An hour later Penny was on the mean streets in her street person disguise. Two hours later she had located a pimp with a stable of young girls, all under the age of twelve.

By morning the police were frantic. They had four dead pedophiles, one dead pimp, three more pimps in hospital with various injuries, and a half dozen badly abused girls needing help. It was madness. The only good thing was the Chosen had voluntarily left town.

Back at the campsite they were settling down for a rest. Suddenly Penny sat up with a start. "Thunder, where's Ryder?"

He sighed as he settled down under a tree. "She'll be along soon. She had an errand to run."

"Jesus, Thunder, Kara will skin the lot of us if anything happens to her. Where did she go?"

"She recognized a place, said she was going to visit an old friend, if you get my drift. Kyle and Marla went with her. She'll be fine, Blue. She's sixteen and tough as nails. Hell, I'd been on my own three years by then."

"I hear bikes," said Mai. They turned to where she pointed to see three riders coming in. One was carrying a passenger.

"That was real good, Ryder," grinned Kyle, as they all dismounted. "Looks like you're all good carrying passengers now. How did it feel?"

"The bike felt heavy at first," she replied, "but it only took a few minutes to get the feel of it. What'd you think, Grace?"

"It was fun," replied the girl. "Is she here?"

"Not yet, it'll take a few days for her to get here. You can hang out with us until she gets back, right Thunder?"

"Sure thing. You did say her name is Grace. She the one we're looking for?"

"Yup, her uncle's a cop in Seattle."

"You not in a hurry to get home, Grace?"

The girl's face crumpled and she burst into tears. "They might not want me. I've been ruined."

"Hey now, none of that," soothed Ryder as she took the girl in her arms. "Come on now, I promised to introduce you to the real Lady Blue. She's right here. Come on."

Penny was on her feet now. "Come here to me, Grace." The girl fell into those welcoming arms and sobbed her heart out.

When the storm of emotion passed she untangled herself from Penny's arms. "Sorry."

"It's okay. Come and sit with me. Tell me how you met up with our favorite rough Ryder."

The girl sat close to Penny and Mai. "It was the craziest thing. We were all locked up, as usual, waiting for a master to come pick one of us. We heard Master Louie yell something, he sounded scared. We could head fighting and Louie screaming, and then he was crying and talking to mistress Ryder, begging her not to kill him.

"Anyway, it got quiet then the door opened and she was there, unhooking the chains and letting us go. She asked for me and brought me with her. They called the cops to save the other girls."

Penny nodded thoughtfully then looked at Ryder. "Okay, Blue, I'll talk. I saw that bastard run when the Chosen showed up on the street. I recognized him and went after him. I took off so fast Kyle and Marla followed to see what was up.

"Louie tried to hide, but I knew where I was by then and Kyle kicked the door in for me, but they stayed out of it when I fought him.

"That guy had me for over a year, and loved to use the whip on me. If the customer wasn't happy, I got whipped, if one of the other girls fussed, I got whipped. He hated me because he couldn't break me.

"He's got a bad knee, so I went for that. I took him down and twisted that leg 'til he couldn't scream any more, then I let the girls out. I heard two shots. When I turned around he was dead with a gun in his hand."

"The chickenshit tried to back shoot her, Blue," said Kyle. "I had to plug him." Penny nodded her approval.

"Anyway," Ryder went on, "we found Grace in the group, so I offered her a ride on my bike. She didn't trust my driving, so I had to promise to introduce her to Lady Blue and the Fallen Angel."

Ryder turned to Kyle. "Now, we have an issue, Kyle."

"We do?"

"He was mine, Kyle. All you had to do was yell a warning. I could have taken him, and I wanted to. You shot him to protect me from having to do it myself."

For once Kyle didn't play the joker. "There's no way back from that, Ryder. Remember what Blue told you about why we do what we do."

She met his eyes for a long moment then lightly punched his arm. "It's about saving the girls, not about payback. Okay, I get it. The thing is, it scares me how badly I wanted to do it, pay him back for what he did to me, to everybody. Thanks, buddy."

Kyle grinned. "So, want a beer?"

"That stuff tastes like shit. Penny, you got any ginger ale?"

"Sure do. Want one, Grace?" she nodded.

Grace sipped at the ginger ale for a while then spoke. "Ryder, what are you guys going to do with me now?"

"Do with you? Girl, I have no idea at all what to do with you. I wanted to find you and I did. The rest is up to you."

"I don't know what to do, and I'm scared. I ..."

"Easy, easy girl, it's okay. Penny, help me here."

Penny smiled and put her arm around the distraught girl's shoulders. "How about you be my sidekick for a few days until you figure out what you want to do."

"Your sidekick?"

"Yeah, you know, hang out with me, ride with me on the bike, stuff like that. We can talk about stuff and make Kyle go buy us more ginger ale. Grace, you need time to sort out some things in your mind. This is all new and you need time to process it a bit.

"Come on, snuggle down here for a while and get some sleep. You've had a long night." The girl settled down beside Penny and Marla laid a blanket over her. She was soon asleep.

As soon as the girl was sleeping soundly Penny rose and approached Ryder, Marla, Kyle, and Thunder. "Guys, we can't keep her, we have to get her home."

"I know," said Thunder. "This is crazy shit, and the craziest part is she's scared to death of us."

"It's because she's broken," said Ryder. "She wasn't strong enough, and he broke her."

"What'd you mean?" asked Marla.

Ryder sighed then relaxed back. "They all try to break you. When you break, they become your family, your safe place. You won't try to escape, you just take the punishment the johns dish out because you know, at the end, they have to take you back to the pimp where you feel safe. He keeps you fed, gives you clothes and stuff, and as long as you please him you're safe.

"Now Grace is all fucked up because we killed the man who she felt safe with. Yes, she hated him and the things he let other men do to her, but still he was the one she felt safe with.

"She might even think she was doing things for the johns because that would make Louie pleased with her. It's sick shit, but it is what it is. He tried to break me, but he couldn't. They all tried, but they couldn't do it."

"Why was that, Ryder?" asked Thunder.

"Because I was already broken before I was slaved out. I knew what they were doing. It was my foster father who broke me, but watching the pimps work on other girls showed me how it worked, what he'd done to me, what they were trying to do. Once you know how it works, they can't break you anymore because you know the lie in it.

"Penny's right, Thunder, we can't keep her."

"All right, so what do we do here, Blue?"

"We give her a few days to mull it over until Kara gets back. Once Ryder keeps the promise to introduce her then we make a plan to put her back with her family if possible."

Her phone buzzed then and she glanced at it. "Kara's just leaving Denver now. I'll let her know we have Grace." She sent the text then sighed.

"Get some sleep, Blue," said Thunder. "You and Mai had a busy night last night, too."

"Yeah, we did."

———— ◉ ————

THE BIG POLICEMAN GLANCED down at his personal phone. It was a long distance call from Denver. "Yes?"

"It's Angel. Grace is alive and with the Chosen. I'll call again in a couple of days."

"Oh thank god. I owe you more than you know."

"Okay, have you ever heard of a pedophile operating out of the LA area named Albert?"

"No, can't say that I have, but I can ask around."

"Don't, that will just arouse suspicion. Grace is safe with the Chosen for now. We'll get her back to you, I promise. I'll call again in a couple of days."

The line went dead and he slipped the phone back into his pocket. For a long time after that he sat in his car, lost in a turmoil of emotions. The mad serial killer and her bike gang had done what his precious system couldn't. Grace was still alive and now safe with the Chosen.

With any luck he would soon be able to bring her home. He decided to say nothing to anyone, not even his sister, until he had the child safely back in his arms.

Later that night, as he lay trying to sleep, his mind refused to stop churning the situation over, worrying at it like a dog with a bone. They'd found pieces of twenty-three bodies in that man's backyard. Twenty-three young lives snuffed out after enduring hours of brutal torture.

What had him twisted around so badly was they had suspected him of being a pedophile for a long time, but under the rules, their hands were tied. The Fallen Angel had kicked in his door, tore the truth from him, and then put a permanent stop to his murdering ways.

And yet, by the rules he had sworn to uphold, he was duty bound to stop her. At length he sighed deeply. "Ah, fuck it, I've got my twenty years in. I'll take that early retirement, spend a few years trying to make it up to Grace and her mother for my failure to protect her. I'm sick of protecting the rights of scum like that."

With that decision made, he finally drifted off into a troubled sleep.

Many miles away, someone else was having trouble sleeping. Kara tossed and turned as she fought the demon in her head. Each time sleep claimed her it brought her dreams of the things she had endured, the torture, humiliation, the rapes, all of it.

Kara had been able to withstand the pain, she had learned to shut off her mind when her body was invaded, but it was the humiliation that burned the hottest, screaming out for revenge.

"Make them pay," hissed the voice of darkness in her mind. "You're the strongest, not them. You are the master, they are the vermin beneath your feet. Crush them and rejoice in their screams. Grind them beneath your heel."

"I will if you just shut the fuck up and let me sleep," she snarled.

"As you wish, but don't forget who it was who showed you the true path to power, who it was who gave you permission to seek the vengeance you so richly deserve."

"Yeah, yeah, rah, rah, just let me rest, dammit." It did, at last. As she drifted off Kara silently vowed to get full revenge for everything. The demon had no idea it was also on her hit list. It had severed her connection to her goddess, and for that it would have to pay. The Fallen Angel had her own agenda.

Two days later the Chosen were at a bar in LA when Kara walked in. At first there were hoots and cat calls until Ryder recognized her. "Angel!" She grabbed Kara in a hug and was swinging her around and around.

"Put me down, you crazy woman, you're killing me." Laughing, Ryder put her down then grabbed her hand and dragged her outside. "Where are we going?"

"Playground across the street. Come on, I promised Grace I'd introduce you."

"You dumped her in a playground?"

"No, no, Penny and Mai are hanging out with her. She can't go in the bar, you know that."

"Didn't stop you."

"Yeah, but I'm special."

Kara laughed at that. "Oh yeah, what makes you so damn special?"

"My big sister is the Fallen Angel, and I ride with the Chosen. That gives me status. Come on, there they are. Hey guys, look who I found."

They all looked up and smiled. Mai gave Kara a wolf whistle too. "Wow, Angel, you clean up right nice, you do. Come give me a hug, pretty girl."

"Are you going to grab my ass?"

"Oh hell yes."

"Then you stay over there."

Mai burst out laughing and opened her arms. Kara gave her a hug then turned to Penny. "Hey there, big sister, who's your buddy?"

"This is Grace," replied Penny as she gave Kara a hug. "Grace, this is Kara."

"Hi there, Lady Grace, we've been looking everywhere for you. I'm glad they found you in one piece."

"Yeah," she replied shyly, "more or less."

"I get that," said Kara, as she sat on the bench beside the girl. "Go ahead, I can see it in your eyes."

"Huh?"

"Go ahead and ask, it's okay."

The girl grinned sheepishly and looked down. "Sorry. I guess I was expecting you to look different."

"You mean bigger, fiercer, taller even?"

"Yeah, that. I mean, everybody is scared to death of you, and ..."

"It's the dress and heels, right? That's what's messing it up? Stay right there, I won't be long."

Kara stood and fairly danced across the street to a car. She took a small bag from the trunk then disappeared into the bar. There was another round of whistles and cat calls as she entered. She gave them the finger and disappeared into the washroom.

A moment or two later she re-emerged wearing her leathers and Chosen colors. Outside she tossed the bag back into the car and ran across the street to plop down beside Grace. "Better?"

"More like what I expected, but you didn't have to do that for me."

"I didn't, those damned heels were killing me. Give me a good sturdy boot any day. So, what's the scoop here, are you ready to go home?"

"Not yet. Penny said I could hang out with her for a few days. Is that okay to do?"

"Up to you and Penny, girl. I'm not your momma. Listen, there's a guy up in Seattle who says he's your uncle. The man really wants to see you."

"He won't when he finds out what happened to me, the things I've done. None of them will. God, I can just see their faces."

Kara sighed and put an arm around the girl's shoulders. "I felt the same way when Penny brought me out. It was a scary, crazy time. You need a few days to sort things out a bit. I get that. Will you do me one favor though?"

"What's that?"

"Talk to your uncle. I need to call him to let him know you're safe. Will you talk to him for a minute?"

"Well, okay, I guess."

"Hey, it's all right, it's just a phone, you don't like what you're hearing then you pass it back to me, okay?"

"Penny and Ryder are right, you're pretty cool."

"I have my good days. So, I call him?" The girl nodded so Kara made the call.

"Angel?"

"I've got somebody here who wants to say hello. You go easy, okay?"

"I will, I swear."

Kara passed the phone to Grace and walked away. Penny, Ryder, and Mai joined her.

A while later the girl came to them and passed back the phone. "He says he's quit the police force. He's got five more days to work then he's coming down here to get me. Can I stay with you guys until then?"

"Of course you can," grinned Penny, as she gently hugged the girl's shoulders. "I'm in no hurry to lose my sidekick."

"Fine," grinned Kara, "you guys hang out here if you want, I'm going for a beer."

She walked back to the bar and went inside. "All right, which one of you monkey faces was laughing at me in heels?"

"Have a beer, Angel," grinned Kyle, "you're too grouchy." He made room for her at the table and passed her a glass.

Tracking a Killer

M orning found Kara focused on her phone. Penny returned from the facilities and started the campfire going again. The others were beginning to stir as well. "What's so interesting, sis?"

"Huh?"

"Sorry to break your concentration," smiled Penny, as she started cooking breakfast. "I just wondered what was so interesting?"

"I'm looking for stories of suddenly missing girls in this general area. Anything official would be too old to be useful. I need the right now stuff."

"Okay, so where do you find that, news reports?"

"Some, but Facebook or Twitter mostly."

"Gods, Kara, I never thought of tracking these guys that way."

"I'm not sure if we can," sighed Kara, dropping the phone onto the ground beside her. "What I'm looking for is girls who've suddenly gone missing, maybe see if we can narrow down the area we need to comb through. We know Merle's hunting, we also know he's desperate, so anything that shows up in the past few days might be a lead.

"We've got to go after the johns and pimps here again, see if we can't beat something useful out of them. Hell, Penny, I'm wide open to suggestions, anything at all. I really want to find these bastards. Every time I think of those pictures I want to kill something, anything to make it stop."

"We'll find them, sis, we'll find them. Here, have some breakfast before you start on the beer."

"Ha, ha, ha, very funny." Penny passed her a plate and she tucked in with a will. "Thanks, Penny, that was great."

"Sure. Kara, hang out with us today. When it gets dark we'll leave Ryder and a few others here to protect Grace and the rest of us will go hunting."

"Works for me. Maybe I'll check in with Arlo, see if he's got anything for me." Penny nodded as Kara picked up her phone and called.

"Arlo."

"It's Angel, got anything for me?"

"Just my heartfelt thanks. Jesus, Angel, the bastard grabbed Keisha right out of a group getting on a bus. He threw her in the trunk of his car, but she kicked out the taillights and stuck her hand out the hole and waved. One of the other guys saw it and pulled him over. They got her back.

"Angel, she told me later you taught her that. I owe you more than you know."

"Just help me find these bastards so I can kill them. Arlo, tell Keisha I'm proud of her."

Kara dropped the phone into her pocket and sighed. "You guys hear that?" both Mai and Penny nodded. "These bastards get bolder every day."

"Yeah, they do," said Penny. "It's our job to stop as many as we can."

"What the hell is this country coming to anyway?"

"The dark is winning, sister mine. Please stop helping it. Come back to Moragah, help us to do this the right way."

"I've told you already, I have tried. Dozens of times, but I can't hear Her or feel Her anymore."

"Nor will you as long as you let that thing in your head keep you blind. You can beat that thing, Kara, I know you can."

"Yeah, sure. Look, are you going to keep this up all day? If you are I'll go hang out with Kyle instead."

"Okay, sweetie, I'll stop preaching." Penny grinned and took the plates and frying pan to the stream for cleaning.

When she returned Grace was awake. They all spent the day wandering the hiking trails and avoiding the main topic on their minds. As the day began to fade Kara became restless. "Okay guys, I guess it's time to get the show on the road. I need a few volunteers to stay here with Grace to keep her safe."

"She can ride with me," said Thunder. "I'll keep an eye on her. Come on, Grace, let's get you into some leather."

Kara watched them walk away; an eyebrow quirked in their direction. "She's broken, Angel," said Ryder. "If you leave her here with me and a few others she might freak. She knows Thunder is the leader, and she knows he's the strongest. She'll feel safe with him and stick to him like glue."

"Thunders knows this, doesn't he?"

"Yeah."

"You tell him?"

"Yeah, I did."

"Good job, little sis, good job. All right guys, we've got work to do." Motorcycles began to roar to life and move out towards the city. Kara sighed with relief as the speed created a breeze to combat the heat. Damn, she hated the heat.

This night was different, and somehow the streets sensed that. The Chosen didn't stop at a bar, they just slowed down and crawled through the bad parts of town. Sometimes they stopped to talk to someone, a couple of times they caught a pimp and interrogated him.

"Please don't kill me ..." begged the terrified man.

"Just shut up and pay attention," said Thunder. "Now, in honesty, I don't give a shit how you or your girls make a living, I don't, just as long as the girls are in the business of their own free will. That and they're a bunch older than this girl sitting behind me.

"Take a long hard look at her, note how young she is. Now, tell me who has a stable of girls about that age."

"I can't. He'll kill me ..." Thunder raised his arm and made a motion in the air. A motorcycle moved out of the pack and approached slowly. The rider was a small woman, no helmet, just a faceless mask. The pimp realized who it was and wet himself.

She pulled up beside Thunder and shut off the bike. "This guy knows something, Angel, but he's a bit tight-lipped."

She swung her leg over the bike and stepped towards the cowering man. "You have three options here," she said, her voice cold and death dancing in her eyes.

"Option one, tell me what I want to know, and I go away. Option two, lie to me and suffer pain like you've never dreamed of, and then you tell me anyway. Option three, try something stupid and die where you stand. Choose wisely."

He stood trembling, his mouth working, but no sound coming out. "I can't hear you."

"Juan, his name is Juan," he managed swallowing hard. "Two blocks that way. Look for a black van with a red racing stripe. Please ..." he stopped begging as she had already turned away from him. To his great relief the bikes turned and moved off in the direction he had indicated.

Two blocks later they spotted the van and moved in. The driver tried to pull away, but the bikes surrounded him, and a dozen guns were aimed at him. One of the riders, a woman, jumped off and ripped the back door off the van. His girls were soon sitting on motorcycles behind dangerous looking men. Those bikes turned and slowly drove away.

While the girls were taken away, a small woman got in the passenger's seat. She was wearing a faceless mask. He began to beg for his life, but she drove a dagger deeply into his leg, then jerked it out to hold it to his throat.

He screamed as the blade pierced his leg then began to sweat as it reached his neck. "The guns, slowly, carefully, pass them out to the man outside." Whimpering, he obeyed while clutching his wounded and bleeding leg.

"Now, tell me about the girls, where do you get them?"

"Some I steal," he gulped, "some I buy."

"Who do you buy from?"

"Different people, different people, please, I need help ..."

"Name one."

"What?"

"Name a man you buy from and tell me where to find him."

He swallowed hard, but didn't speak. She pressed the blade tighter to his throat and he started to babble. "I don't know his name, I just call him Igor. He's a Russian, I think. He's always hanging out at the Moscow Bar, tall guy, dark hair, part Hindu I think, scar on his face. Three blocks that way. If I need a girl or if he's broke he ..."

"Okay, I get it. You ever buy from a man named Merle Downy?"

"Yes, a couple of times. Please."

"Where do I find Merle?"

"I don't know, he finds you. I heard he's in town, but ..."

"Have you ever sold a girl to a man named Albert?"

"No."

"But you know who he is."

"Yes."

"Where do I find him?"

"I don't know, please ..."

"Tell me, where do I find him?"

"I don't know, somewhere north of the city, in the hills, he's got a farm somewhere up there. Oh gods, I don't feel so good, please ..."

She whipped the knife away from his throat and drove it deep into his body below the rib cage, thrusting upwards and slicing through heart and lungs. As his eyes bugged out and life left him, she pulled out the knife and wiped it on his shirt then left the van and mounted her bike.

"We keep looking," she said. The bikes turned and moved out. Her eyes wide with fear, Grace clung tightly to Thunder's jacket.

They found the bar and a number of the riders went in. The place didn't look friendly. Three men dressed in expensive suits approached. "We don't want your kind in here," said the first man.

A small woman wearing a faceless mask stepped forward. "Give me that man," she said pointing to a dark skinned man with a visible scar, "and I'll leave peacefully."

"And if we don't?"

"I'll kill every fucking human in this shit hole, and then burn it to the ground."

He started to say something then one of the others grabbed his arm and spoke in Russian. His face visibly paled. He made a motion with his hand. The dark skinned man made a break for it, but two other men stepped in his way and dragged him back. "Why do you want this scum anyway?"

"I want information, he has it."

"And if he won't talk?"

Fire suddenly blazed up around her, driving the men back. She danced and swirled it in the air then put it out. "Trust me, he'll talk."

Wide-eyed the man grabbed the hapless object of her desire and thrust him towards her. "Take that outside, if you please."

Kyle grabbed the man and hauled him out the door. The rest of the gang followed, but Kara remained between them and the Russians. "I have what I wanted. Are we good here?"

"We have no problems if you don't."

"Then we're good. I apologize for disturbing your evening. As long as we're good, the Chosen have no reason to return." She suddenly vanished through the open door. The men stood silently listening as the bikes roared to life and moved away.

"How can she do that with fire?"

"Fallen Angel my ass, that one is a demon straight from hell. I need more vodka."

Terrified, the man ran beside her bike. He'd tried to escape twice, but she'd dragged him. He hurt terribly, but she was relentless. Finally she turned into an alley. She shoved him towards the back wall then dismounted and walked towards him.

"Stay away from me," he said as he backed away from her. "What do you want?"

"You capture young girls and sell them, yes?"

"Sometimes." He was still backing away.

"Do you know a man named Albert?"

"Yes, I have sold him girls before."

"How do I find him?"

"You don't. He finds you." She moved closer and he gasped in fear as his back hit the wall behind him. "I don't know how to find him; he calls when he wants one."

"He calls and you kidnap a girl, then what happens."

"We meet, he pays me and takes her away."

"Where do you meet?"

"Different places. A different place every time. Stay back."

She moved closer. "When he leaves, which way does he go?"

"I don't know, he ..."

He got no further as she leaped at him and sank her fist into his belly, driving the air from his lungs and sending him to the ground. "You're lying, I can see it in your eyes. You've followed him, haven't you?"

"Yes, but he got away," replied the terrified man. "He turned onto the highway north and I lost him in the traffic."

"Piece of shit," she muttered, as she walked away and got back on her bike. Grace tightened her grip on Thunder as Kara turned and sent a blast of hellfire at the predator. He screamed and screamed as he burned, but she held the fire on him until he died.

The night was growing late, and they hadn't gone far when the rest of the gang found them. "You get the kids safely to the cops?" asked Thunder.

"We did," replied Penny. "You guys learn anything?"

"Yeah, some," he replied. "Hey, Angel, we done for the night, or do we keep going?"

"We're done for now. Let's go back to the campsite and catch some rest." The big bikes turned and roared out of town.

Working it Out

"So, you learned something, care to share," said Penny, as they relaxed in the campsite.

"Sure," replied Kara as she caused the cold campfire to leap back to life. "We learned, from two different sources, that Albert has his death camp in the hills north of the city, at least that's as far as anybody's been able to track him. When he wants a victim he contacts some scum or other and places an order. They meet in the city, he takes delivery, and then vanishes on the highway north.

"From what we know, and what we've just confirmed, I'd say we're in the wrong city. I'm thinking he's somewhere between here and Bakersfield, probably closer to Bakersfield, maybe even a bit north of it."

"That would make sense," said Mai as she stretched out beside the small fire. "If he's close to Bakersfield he wouldn't want to hunt there and raise possible suspicion. He'd hunt in LA."

"That was my thought," sighed Kara.

"So we ride north?"

"Yep, first we sleep, and then we ride north." Just as she too stretched out, Kara took out her phone and called.

"Arlo."

"It's Angel. Tell me something good."

"I'm teaching a 'how to not get caught by kidnappers' course in the school. Keisha's helping me by telling her story. We're leaving out any reference to you, of course."

"Right. Got anything about Albert?"

"Got a few hits on that. I'd say your best bet is Bakersfield."

"That jives with what we've learned. Arlo, be careful."

"Promise." The connection broke and Kara sighed. She placed another call.

"Angel? Is Grace okay?"

"Grace's is fine. The Chosen will be heading for Bakersfield later today. Grace will be with them. You want to head south and meet up with us?"

"Oh god yes."

"All right, I'll call again day after tomorrow." She broke the connection then sighed as she lay back.

"You okay, sis?" asked Penny.

"I am, yes, but Grace is a bit fucked up from what she saw me do last night. It wasn't pretty, but it had the desired effect. I got the information, and those scummy bastards will never hurt another child. It works."

"Yeah, I agree, but you're right, we need to get her back to her family, the sooner the better."

"Amen to that," sighed Kara, as she drifted off to sleep.

As Kara went to sleep, frightened eyes watched her from across Thunder's sleeping form. He was stretched out beside his bike with Grace and Ryder close by. Seeing the fear on Grace's face, Ryder took pity on her. "Hey girl, you okay?"

"Yeah, I guess."

"Liar." Ryder reached over to gently pat her shoulder. "Angel freaked you out last night, didn't she?"

"Yeah, I guess."

"Was it where she burned that guy?"

"Yeah. I guess I expected her to shoot him or something, but the way he screamed in the fire freaked me out. She shouldn't have done that, he told her what she wanted to know."

"Seriously? You think she should have let him go?"

"Well, no, but give him to the police maybe? I don't know, I just can't get the screams out of my mind."

"Grace, that fucker made girls like us scream like that, lots of us, and some of them got killed by that Albert guy. Do you remember what it was like the first time? When you were taken from your family and raped, whipped ..."

"Yeah, I remember, but my family wasn't strong enough, they couldn't protect me ..."

"The slavers weren't either, Grace. Remember how easy Angel took them down."

"Yeah, she did, but ..."

"But what?"

"She's not human, is she? She a fallen angel, right?"

"Yeah, sort of, I guess. So?"

"She respects Thunder, all the Chosen."

"That's because they're family."

"And they're strong, like she is. You're lucky, Ryder. You get to stay with them where they can protect you. She likes you, so she'll let you stay. She's going to send me back to my weak family. It'll just be a matter of time before they start to ignore me again and another master grabs me. Maybe even a meaner one than the last time."

"Okay, I get it now. Look, I'll talk to Marla, get her to show you a few tricks. I'll talk to Penny and Mai too. They can teach you stuff to help you stay out of the hands of the masters. I'd ask Angel, but I know you're scared of her, so I won't. We've got a day or two more to work on it if you want to."

"Thanks, Ryder. I'll take all the help I can get."

"Get some sleep, Grace." Ryder sighed as the girl closed her eyes. "Keeping her with us was a mistake," she thought. "If we'd taken her straight back she might have latched onto her uncle as a protector, now she might never get past the idea of Thunder and the Chosen.

"Ah well, not my problem, I guess. Maybe that goddess of Penny's will look out for her." As Ryder drifted off to sleep a wave of gentle loving energy washed over her bringing a smile to her lips.

When Kara awakened she saw Grace and Marla practicing an escape move for when someone has you by the hair. "What's that all about?"

"You scared the shit out of her last night," Ryder replied. "She's afraid to go back to her family because they couldn't protect her from the slavers, and now she knows the masters can't protect her from you.

"You respect the Chosen so she feels safe with us, but she knows you're going to make her go back to the family that couldn't save her. Marla's teaching her a few tricks to help her keep herself free from the slavers, if they ever try to grab her again."

"Shit. Guess I fucked that up, didn't I?"

"Not you, sis, me," said Penny. "Once we had Grace, I should've got that phone number from you and taken her home. You don't get to wear this one, sweetie. I blew this one."

"None of that matters now," said Ryder. "Now we just have to find a way to make her feel safe to go home with Uncle Bill, or whatever the hell his name is."

"You really understand this girl, don't you, Ryder?"

"Yeah, Blue, I do, so does Angel, 'cause we've been there."

"Not quite, little sis," said Kara. "You see through this stuff way better than I do. I'm just a survivor, but you're more, and you're stronger. You look deeper too, into people. This thing with Grace is starting to bug me, what do you recommend we do here?"

Ryder blushed at Kara's praise. "Kara's right, Ryder, you see way more than the rest of us. What should we do here?"

"Well, the problem now is she's starting to latch onto Thunder as the protector. That's why I asked Marla to teach her instead. I think she should ride with somebody different every time we hit the road. That might spread it out a bit and make it easier for her uncle."

"She's right," agreed Penny. "If the girl gets focused on Thunder that's just going to make it harder for her."

"Or worse."

"What do you mean, worse, Mai?" asked Kara.

"If she's crushing on Thunder she could run away and try to hook up with the Chosen again."

"She's right," agreed Ryder. "That could happen."

"Not good," sighed Kara. "Ryder, you clue Thunder in, and then we should get on the road. We've got a long way to go before dark."

Grace rode behind Marla that day. When the gang set up camp at a campsite outside Bakersfield she stayed behind with Marla, Kyle, and a half dozen others while the rest rode into the city and headed for a well known biker bar.

The place was nearly full as they arrived. The bouncer looked like he might say something as Ryder and Kara walked in, but, at a signal from the owner he held his peace. The bartender was a hard looking woman in her fifties. She turned to face them as they approached.

"Hey, Thunder, long time, no see. What are you losers up to these days?"

"This is it," he grinned in reply. "What you see is what you get."

"One of those two kids with you the Fallen Angel?"

"There's no kids here, we left them back at the hotel with the servants."

"Ah-huh. Thunder, I don't want any trouble with the Chosen or the cops. Those two got ID?"

"Yup, they do."

"Okay, I saw the ID and it looked good. Beer all round."

"Yes ma'am. Oh, Linda, I'd keep my hands away from that panic button, you know, just so one of the kids doesn't get nervous, if you know what I mean."

"Yeah, Mickey told me about that."

"You talked to Mickey? He have a message for me?"

"He said the gold is in the hills outside Bakersfield. Said you'd know what it meant."

"Ah-huh. He say where in those hills in particular?"

"Nope. Thunder, just what are you looking for?"

Kara stepped closer and reached for a beer. "We're looking for a pedophile who owns a pig farm. He likes to buy girls about ten or twelve years old and when he's done with them he slaughters them with the pigs."

The woman's face had gone ashen. "You're serious."

Kara took a drink of beer then slid an envelope of pictures across the bar. The woman looked then began to shake and fight to keep her stomach down. "Sweet Jesus Christ, I didn't need to see that."

"Yes you did," replied Kara. "Now you know what we're hunting, and why."

"You're the Fallen Angel, aren't you? God, woman, I hope you find that animal and I hope it takes him days to die."

"Oh yeah, I'll find him, and when I do he's going straight to hell. His name's Albert, mean anything to you?"

"No, sorry, I wish it did."

"How about Merle Downy?"

"Nope. I'll keep my eyes and ears open though; I swear it." Kara nodded and turned away, but the woman's voice called her back. "Angel, don't waste a lot of time finding that bastard."

"You lost somebody, didn't you?"

"A long time ago, but ..."

Kara nodded. "I won't waste time, I promise. I'll find him, and he'll pay the price." The bartender nodded then handed back the photos. Kara tucked them in her pocket and went to her table. A while later a matchbook landed beside her.

Kara thumbed it open and found an address inside. She looked up to see the bartender standing beside her. "There's a pig farm there. Don't know if it's the right one. I'll see if I can locate more." Kara thanked her as she walked away.

The next morning three young women in a stolen car approached the farm. A woman and a passel of youngsters were in the yard. This wasn't the place they were looking for, and the owners didn't know of another farmer called Albert. They apologized and drove away.

The gang was waiting for them on the highway with their bikes. They pulled on their leathers then abandoned the car and rode away.

"Well, what now?" asked Kyle, as they sat in the roadside cafe having lunch.

"Damned if I know," replied Kara. "I'm wide open to suggestions."

"He's a pig farmer," said Penny. "We're going about this the wrong way."

"Okay, enlighten me," said Kara.

"Albert the killer is secretive beyond all measure, right?"

"Right," replied Kara, taking a sip of her coffee.

"Well, maybe Albert the farmer isn't so secretive. He has to buy feed for his animals, doesn't he? When he sends them to market he has to hire trucks, doesn't he?"

"I get the impression by those pictures that he does the slaughtering himself."

"Okay, then his place needs to be inspected by the health authorities. The inspectors must know his name and where his farm is."

Kara just shook her head and grinned. "Gods you're good. That's why I always called you the brains of the outfit, Penny. Okay, people, my face is a bit too well known to the authorities, I'd rather not try this on my own in daylight. Any of you willing to give a girl a hand at some detective work?"

There was a round of laughter at that. "Sure, Angel, you take the day off tomorrow while we go play Kojak and see if we can locate this fucker."

"Thunder, you guys are too good to me." There was another round of chuckles at that.

The next morning the gang rode out heading into the city to find the feed stores. Penny went shopping, then changed herself back into Penny Larson before heading into the government offices.

While they were gone, Grace stayed in the campsite with Kara and Mai. Kara called her uncle and insisted she talk to him. It was a stiff conversation and didn't go well. Kara promised him they'd call back the next day to make arrangements for him to pick her up.

"Grace, I know this is going to be tough, but you've got to go home with him," said Mai.

"I really don't want to. I thought he'd come to get me. He's a policeman and I was always taught, … I mean I believed he would come to rescue me, but he didn't. I …" She burst into tears and Mai held her as she cried.

When the storm of emotion passed, Kara spoke. "I know exactly how you feel, girl. I felt the same."

"You? What do you mean? How could you know how I feel?"

"Because I was you, Grace. I thought you knew I was taken like you."

"I didn't know that. How could anyone take you?"

"I was human back then. Okay, I was taken and used for over three years before Penny dug me out and trained me. When she took me home I had to face my grandfather who hadn't come to save me. My dad had left my mom a year after I was taken, and I still don't know where the hell he is, but I do know he didn't come for me either.

"Grace, they couldn't come for us because they couldn't find us. They don't know how. If they'd been able to find us they'd have come, or at least they'd have tried."

"Do you really believe that?"

"Yes I do, girl. The problem is, they don't have the skills to find us, and they have to play by the rules, especially the cops. Now, your uncle, he's not a cop anymore. He doesn't have to play by the rules now, and I'm pretty damn sure he won't. I'd give him a chance if I were you."

"Yeah? Well, maybe, I guess." The girl looked thoughtful, and they left her to it.

———●———

WHILE EVERYBODY WAS out looking for Albert's farm and Kara was trying to convince Grace to go back to her family, Merle Downy was hunting, stalking his prey. This was going to be tough because he needed two, and he needed them now.

He was sweating as he watched the convenience store. People came and went, but no opportunity presented itself. Merle was desperate for a drink, or a toke, but he dare not, not while on the hunt.

Dammit, he hated this. He was too far away from safety, and it had been over a week of sleeping in his car. Nobody would take him in, they were too afraid of the Fallen Angel.

Jesus, pretty little Kara. What the fuck had happened to make her the Fallen Angel? She'd been tough, able to take lots of pain, but this was crazy. Somehow she'd found a way to make a deal with the devil. They said she was strong as a dozen men now, and she could shoot fire from her hands.

That was crazy talk, it had to be. Merle pulled out another cigarette and lit it, taking a long deep drag and holding it in his lungs for a moment to calm his nerves. Shit, only three cigs left, and his money was gone. Worse, he barely had enough gas to get back to Albert's place.

Albert, now there was a sick bastard, but for a price he'd hide Merle, and Merle needed to raise that price.

Suddenly he sat up straight. There she was, just what he needed, a young brunette about eleven or twelve years old. She was following a few paces behind her mother, staring at the phone in her hands, her thumbs flying. The mother was talking constantly over her shoulder, but the child was ignoring her. Merle practically drooled as he watched them enter the store.

Trying not to look like he was in a rush, Merle moved his car over beside the mother's SUV. Taking his time, he got out of the car and opened his trunk. There was a suitcase there and another case as well. That one held what he needed.

Making sure no one was watching, and keeping his back to the street cameras, Merle took out wrist and ankle restraints and a ball gag. He stuffed them into his pockets then closed the case and put it in the back seat of the car. The suitcase followed.

His heart began to race as he watched the mother and daughter return to their vehicle. For a brief moment he thought about taking them both, but the woman was too old, Albert would never go for that. He continued to fuss in the trunk of his car as they approached.

The woman unlocked her car then opened the back. She was looking inside and yakking away to her offspring, but not really paying attention to the girl. As Merle had hoped, the girl remained a few steps behind her mother, still completely focused on her phone.

Her mother was still talking and putting the purchases in the back of the car when a hand clamped down hard on the girl's mouth. She made a startled squeak, but a strong arm swept her into the air and deposited her in the trunk of a car. She screamed as the lid was slammed down.

At the sound of her daughter's scream the woman turned around. A fist cracked against her jaw and her purse was snatched as she melted to the ground. She was trying to shake off the cobwebs as the car raced away carrying her screaming child.

The girl screamed, cried, and kicked at the back of the trunk, but all to no avail. Frantically she searched for her phone, but she'd dropped it when she'd been grabbed. Eventually she stopped kicking and screaming and just cried her heart out. She was still wailing when the car stopped.

She trembled in fear as she heard the man's steps approaching the trunk. The lid popped open and she tried to kick at him. He batted her foot aside and slapped her hard across the face. She was in shock as he grabbed her hair and dragged her halfway out of the car.

A ball of some kind was forced into her mouth and secured with a strap behind her head. It was big and it hurt her mouth. She tried to kick again, but he grabbed her hair and jerked her close to him.

"You be still, do as you're told, and I might let you live. You piss me off and I'll give you to old Albie. He'll cut your throat, gut you like a pig, and then skin you out. He'll make sausages out of you and eat them, that's after he's done torturing you.

"If you behave yourself I'll train you to be a good girl and sell you to a pimp, but at least you'll still be alive. Now you be still, and I won't hurt you too much right now."

Terrified, she stopped trying to struggle. Her wrists were secured behind her back, her ankles secured then locked to her wrists. He squeezed her young breast a few times and grinned his approval before stuffing her back into the trunk and dropping the lid.

Back in the front, Merle searched the woman's purse. Jesus, only forty-five dollars and some change. Shit, everybody uses the damned bank cards these days. Nobody carries cash anymore. Swearing profusely, Merle headed for a gas bar and put the whole forty-five into the tank. He needed the gas more than the beer.

The one in the trunk was being quiet so he continued the hunt. It was growing late when he finally spotted another good possibility. Three young teenage girls walked down the street towards the small convenience store he had staked out.

"Are you sure you'll be okay?"

"Sure. My house is just down the block, and the streets are well lit. I'll just pick up some snacks then go straight home. I'll phone you when I get in." All music to Merle's ears.

He slipped into the store behind the girl, keeping his hat down over his eyes. Merle was tired, nervous, and getting the shakes. He was also getting desperate and thus, sloppy. It was obvious he was watching the girl. He also stood too close to her at the counter.

Suddenly a gun appeared at his head and the woman's voice sounded cold and dangerous. "Y'all want to be stepping back from this gal now, you hear? Step back."

Merle swallowed hard as the gun pressed against his forehead and the object of his desire slipped away from him. Again the woman's voice sounded close. How the hell had she gotten around the counter that fast anyway. She was admonishing the girl to hurry home.

The woman made only one mistake, but it was enough. Her eyes darted to the girl as the door closed behind her, and in that moment Merle struck. He batted the gun aside and landed a solid punch to the face, knocking the woman unconscious.

As she fell he bolted through the door after the girl. Sadly, she had stopped to call the police. The dispatcher was still on the line when the girl screamed and was carried away.

A few hard slaps to the face subdued his victim then she was deposited in the trunk with the first one. Merle hurried behind the wheel then slowly drove away. Two police cars went screaming by towards the convenience store as Merle headed for the highway.

It was a long drive to Albert's place outside Bakersfield. He hoped he had enough gas to make it. He stopped only once to secure the second capture and gag her. Shit, he had a fortune in his trunk and he dared not sell them. He needed sanctuary and Albert's was the only place where the Angel wouldn't be able to find him.

The sun was already up as the old car left the narrow country road and crawled up the long dusty driveway. A man with a shotgun emerged from the house and waited for the car to arrive at the old house. As the car reached him he peered at the driver and set his shotgun aside then sat on the top step.

"Is that you, Merle?"

"Hey, Albert, how's it going?"

"Shitty. Been a dry year and the price of feed went way the hell up. I've had to spend every dollar on this damned farm. Haven't had a cent to my name all year. I don't suppose you brought me a present, did you? I'm dying for a little fun."

"Just so happens I did. I've got two in the trunk. Albie, I'm flat broke and on the run. I need a place to hide out and train one of them for sale. You can have the other one if you let me stay."

"Now, I heard that the Fallen Angel is on your trail, is that right? Seems to me I'd be taking an awful chance, hiding you from that character."

"She's a demon from hell, Albie. God's truth. Look, we're friends and you know you can trust me. You let me stay and give me time to train one. As soon as I sell her I'll catch a couple more, one for you to play with and we can split the money for the second one. Will that work for you?"

The older man nodded thoughtfully for a moment. He knew it was a big risk, but it had been so long, and there was a fresh one right in front of him. "Let me see 'em, see what you got."

Merle popped the lid on the trunk and light flooded in on the two bound girls. He walked back and pulled them out by the hair, standing them up for Albert to inspect. Both girls tried to jerk away, but Merle yanked them back.

"You behave yourselves and stand still. You're not spoiled little girls anymore, you're slaves now. You do as you're told when you're told, and only what you're told. We'll touch you any time and anywhere we want to, and you will be still when we do, or you'll be punished. That's Albie's favorite part and mine too."

Terrified, the two girls tried to be still while Albert inspected them, pinching their nipples and feeling their butts, poking and prodding at their bodies. Both tried to be quiet, but couldn't. Nor could they escape, for they were both bound and gagged.

"Which one do I get, Merle?"

"Your choice, buddy. I just need one to sell and a tank of gas to get back to the city."

"Don't go back to LA, the Angel's there hunting for you. Better off to take her north to sell, get more money for her too. All right, Merle, it's a deal." Suddenly he reached out and pinched one girl's breast hard. She yelped and tried to jerk away, but he gave her a backhand slap across the face, knocking her down.

"I want that one, Merle. She'll squeal right nice for me. Come on, let's put them in the pen then go have some breakfast. You look like you've been up all night. You can sleep while I go to town for feed, we can play with these two later tonight."

Merle unlocked the ankle straps from the girls then led them after Albert's retreating back. They'd been cramped up too long and stumbled often, but each time he grabbed them by the hair and jerked them back to their feet.

They entered the barn; Albert took a broom and swept a piece of the floor then pulled a remote from his pocket. The slab of concrete lifted up and moved aside, revealing a set of stairs below. He started down and flicked the lights on.

The two girls found themselves in a torture chamber. There were whips, chains, paddles, canes, knives, assorted benches and cages, and a lot more. "I've only got the one stocks, so you'll have to tie yours up someplace else. I want a little something to start my day off right." So saying Albert dragged the girl he'd chosen to the stocks.

"Get those clothes off," he commanded, as he released her wrists. She tried to run, but he caught her by the hair, a knife appearing in his hand. "Get 'em off or I'll cut up that pretty face of yours." Terrified, she obeyed. "Now, get your head in there like a good little piggy."

Her head and wrists were placed in the stocks and the wooden bar lowered. He locked it then checked to make sure she couldn't get out. Grinning, he unhooked the gag and pulled it from her mouth. "I like to hear my piggies squeal a bit."

He knelt and grabbed her ankle. She tried to kick at him, but he was too strong. Her leg was pulled aside and her ankle fastened in place.

He then went to the other side and fastened that ankle. She was now bent over, naked, her legs spread apart and secured. He stepped behind her and she screamed as she felt his hands probing at her vagina.

"My god, Merle, you bring me the best presents. This one's a virgin. Oh, you're the best. It's been years since I've had a virgin." Suddenly the girl screamed again as the white hot pain of the rape hit her. He slammed himself into her repeatedly until he groaned and stepped back. She hung in the stocks, crying, blood running down her leg.

"Now then, Merle old buddy, toss that one in the pen and we'll get some breakfast." The second girl had been forced to watch and had vomited. Merle forced her to strip then took her by the hair and tossed her into a cage that was too small for her to stand up in. He locked the door and followed Albert up the stairs.

He still hadn't taken out her gag or released her wrists. Both girls whimpered as the lights went out and they were left in total darkness.

"I gotta tell ya, Merle, that was a true delight. Been a long time since I've had a virgin. Those other assholes bring me used goods, but you always bring me the best."

"I never taste one meant for you, Albie, you know that. I like to train my own because I get a lot more money for a well-trained slave, but I know you like 'em still fresh so I try to get that for you."

"You're a good man, Merle. Best friend this old fool ever had. So, you'll really get me another one?"

"Promise. Give me a couple of weeks to train that one then I'll take it up to Portland and sell it. I'll pick up a couple more on the way back."

Avenging Angel

Penny got nowhere in her quest at the government building, as the inspectors were all out on the job. She left, changed back into biker gear, and rejoined the Chosen.

They'd split up into small groups so they wouldn't scare people at the feed stores. Most of what they wanted was on the edge of town anyway. It was mid-afternoon when Penny caught up with Thunder and Ryder.

"You guys having any luck?"

"Sure," groused Ryder, "all bad. We've been lied to a half dozen times and threatened with the cops twice. Shit, all we did was ask a question."

"Farm folks get nervous around bikers?"

"Apparently so," grinned Thunder. "According to this list, we've got one more place to go then we have to call it a bust. If we come up empty we'll have to start looking at smaller towns close by."

"All right," said Penny as she put her helmet back on, "let's check this last one out. Fingers crossed."

Thunder turned and headed down the long street. It took a while to find the place as it was in an industrial area. They pulled up to the store office and dismounted. The girl behind the counter looked up then took a step back.

Penny shook out her hair and put on her brightest smile. "Hi there."

"Hi yourself, can I help you?"

"Gosh, I sure hope so. I'm looking for someone."

"Okay ..."

"It's funny, in an odd sort of way. I was raised by my grandmother, and she died a few months ago. I just recently found out I have an uncle who lives around here. Apparently he owns a pig farm somewhere, but I can't find an address for him."

"What's his name?"

"Albert."

"Just Albert?"

"I got the information from Gramma's diaries. Albert's the only name I've got. Can you help me? Do you know of any pig farmers around here named Albert?"

The girl shook her head. "No, can't say as I do. You could ask the guys out in the yard though; they know everybody in the area. Right through that door there."

"Cool. Thanks. You guys wait for me at the bikes. I'll just be a minute." She tossed Ryder her helmet then stepped through the back door into the yard.

It was a wide open area confined by a tall heavy wire fence. There were trucks and machinery everywhere. A tall, lanky, youth spotted the pretty girl in leathers and approached with his most winning smile. "Hey there, can I help?"

"Sure. I'm looking for my uncle." Once again Penny repeated her story. "So, do you know of anybody by that name?"

"Sure thing. You just missed him, girl. There he goes now, old yellow truck with a green tarp pulled over the box. He just picked up a load of feed. Sign on the truck says Finkle Farms.

"So, you moving out to these parts?"

Penny gave him her brightest smile. "Ya know, I just might at that. If I do I'll look you up. Sorry, gotta run catch Uncle Albert now." She danced away from him and went back through the office to where Thunder and Ryder were waiting.

"Well?" asked Thunder.

"Got him. He just left, that's him turning the corner down the street." They both turned to look. "The sign on the side says Finkle Farms. You two ride past and double check we have the right guy. If that's the right truck give me a high fist and I'll follow him home. You guys go back to Kara and wait for me.

Thunder nodded then started his engine. The two bikes set out fast, but Penny hung back a bit. As they got out onto the more open road the two bikes roared past the old truck. The riders both gave a raised fist sign then roared away.

Albert took his time, not trying to push the old truck. He was lost in thoughts of the delight he'd experienced that morning and imagining the fun he'd have this night. Merle had brought him a special prize and he planned to take his time with her.

With any luck she'd last for a couple of weeks until Merle got his sold and brought him a new one. Oh yeah, the new one could watch him butcher the old one. Oh god, the idea made him almost orgasm with the thought.

He kept playing it over and over in his mind and never once paid any attention to the lone motorcycle that paced along behind him. Albert arrived home then backed the truck up to the silo and unloaded his cargo. He fed the pigs, then went down to the torture chamber.

Albert chatted away to the girls as he let them out to use the toilet and clean themselves up. He then put them in the small cages and fed them a bowl of slop, the same thing he fed the pigs. He laughed as they looked at it.

"Better eat that, it's all you'll get from now on."

"Please don't do this. Please let us go ..."

"Did I tell you to speak? Did I? One more peep out of you and I'll whip your ass raw. Now eat that or don't, I don't give a shit which." With that he turned on his heel and left.

He flicked off the lights and used the remote to close the lid again, leaving them in total darkness. From a small stand of trees nearby, a pair of cold eyes watched. She'd also heard everything he'd said. Penny slipped back into the trees then returned to her bike at the side of the road. She gunned the engine and raced away.

———————●———————

KARA WAS PACING, AND had been ever since Thunder and Ryder returned. They'd found him. They'd found Albert, and Merle would be with him. Penny was on the trail, no way in hell Albert could shake Lady Blue. Kara was just afraid Penny would take them down alone first. She really wanted to kill Merle herself.

She looked up as the bike roared into the campsite. Penny hopped off and doffed her helmet, shaking out her hair and stretching. "Well?"

"It's him, Kara. He's got two girls in his torture chamber. It's under the barn. You open it with a remote he keeps in his pocket."

"And Merle?"

"I didn't see anybody else, but there's a car in the yard with Virginia plates on it. I did hear someone snoring in the house. I'd say your guy is there."

"Mount up," shouted Kara, as she leaped board her bike.

"Hold on," said Penny.

Kara turned hard eyes on her. "What?"

"This one's it, Kara, the end of the line, just like I promised."

"So?"

"So when it's done, you come back to me, to Moragah. That was the deal."

"Penny, you know ..."

"You promised to try, to let me help you find your way back. We do this then we bring you back, that was the deal. Once you're back with us we'll keep hunting as long as you want, but we hunt Moragah's way, deal?"

Kara sighed and shut off her engine. "Penny, I swear I'll do my best, but I make no promises. I have tried, harder than you might guess. I'll give it everything I've got, I promise I will, but first I get Merle and make him dead for what he did to me. Deal?"

"Deal," replied Penny, as she mounted her bike and started the engine. "Follow me." She spun the bike around and sped away.

As they rode along, being careful to stay within the speed limit, Penny silently called to her goddess. "Lady Moragah?"

"I am here, Penny, my daughter."

"Are we going to be able to do this? Bring Kara back, I mean?"

"We can, Penny, but we need her to truly want to return. The darkness within her is aware of your plan now. Be watchful, for it will try anything to prevent you. It will be trying to drive a wedge between you now.

"We're close, Penny, so close. Now is the time the dark will do something desperate."

"I understand, Lady, I do. I'll keep my eyes open. I just wish I could talk her out of this last piece of revenge. I've got her back to focusing more on freeing the kids than punishing the pedophiles, but I'm afraid this could set her back big time."

"I know, Penny, and I, too, fear this, but we have no other option. This is a risk we have to take. I will do all I can to help you; we must get her away from the darkness. Be watchful and I will as well."

"Thank you, Lady Moragah. I feel better and more hopeful now. I'll stay on my toes, I promise." Moragah pulled back and sent her a wave of loving healing energy. Penny sighed with delight and picked up the speed a bit. The day was getting late.

They pulled off the highway and onto a secondary road. A mile or so more and they reached the farm.

⸻◦⸻

MERLE AWAKENED RESTED for the first time in days. He entered the kitchen to find Albert sitting at the computer. Albert looked up and grinned at Merle. "Just letting the folks know there'll be new pictures coming soon. They're all excited now."

"So are you, by the looks of things. You in a hurry to get started?"

"Nope, the anticipation is half the fun. Let's have something to eat and a beer before we get started."

"Sounds good to me. Did you feed them?"

"Yeah, I did. They're fine. Sweet little piggies."

"Aw, Albie, you gotta feed mine more than that pig slop. I need her strong and healthy or she won't be worth shit on the open market."

"So, you can bring her a pizza or something if you want."

"I'm flat broke until I sell her, Albie, you know that. Don't suppose you could lend me a couple hundred, could you?"

"I'll lend you a hundred. But you pay back double when you sell her."

"Jesus, Albie, you're killing me here."

"Consider it room and board."

"I already paid that."

"Yeah, you did, and she's the best I've had in a lot of years. All right, Merle, I'll lend you three hundred and you pay me back five, deal."

"Deal, you cheap old bugger."

"I told you it was a shitty year. That's about all I've got. So, ham and eggs?"

"That's not human ham, is it?"

"No, I haven't had any of that for a while either, but that'll soon change. This shit is store bought. Will that suit your delicate stomach?"

"It will," sighed Merle, as he sank into a chair at the table. Albert set a beer beside him then started cooking.

The two men sat talking over the meal, Merle regaling Albert with the tale of the hunt and the captures, and Albert soaking it all up. They finished the meal and Albert sat enjoying a second beer while Merle cleaned up.

"Well, looks like it's about time to get things under way," said Albert. "I've never seen anyone train a slave before, you always make me stay in the house. Can I watch this time?"

"Okay, but you can't say anything or touch her."

"How come?"

"Because I need her focused completely on me. Oh she'll squeal plenty for you, sing that pretty song you like, but she has to do it just for me."

"Why?"

"Because if it comes at her from different directions at first it'll ruin her, I need her to keep some of that spirit. Oh, I'll break her alright, but it's like breaking a horse or a dog, they need to know who the master is, only one master. She'll learn to do all sorts of things her mamma doesn't want her to do, and she'll do it all for her master.

"I'm that master and she'll learn to please me, how to squeal and when, what to do and when, and more. It takes about two weeks and then she's ready, she'll do anything at all for her master. When I sell her I make sure she understands he's the new master, and she has to please him like she did me.

"When that happens she'll do anything at all for the freaks who rent her just so her master, the pimp, will be pleased with her.

"Albert, if you touch her or interfere I'll have to start all over and that'll mean feeding me and her for an extra two weeks."

"All right, all right, but I get to watch, it's my dungeon, after all. This'll be something completely new for me. Can I take pictures?"

"Sure, as long as nobody can see my face. Actually, this'll be new for me too. I've never had anybody watch me train one before. You're not thinking about getting into the business, are you?"

Albert laughed at that. "Me? Oh hell no. You know damn well once I get my hands on one I can't ever let anyone else touch them ever again. Have another beer and tell me more about this training thing you do with the little piggies."

Merle stood and brought them each another beer from the fridge. "So, what else do you want to know?" he asked as he resumed his seat.

"Do you do it the same every time, or do you mix it up? What comes first?"

"Oh, the pain comes first. Tie 'em down, make 'em scream until their voice gives out."

"You don't take 'em first?"

"Nope, they have to beg me for that. After a day or two they have it figured out. They scream lots for me and beg to service me then the pain stops. Most of these sick bastards like us enjoy the crying and begging almost as much as the screaming.

"See, right now mine is almost halfway trained. Thanks for that. I might be able to get her market ready in a week if I'm lucky."

"Huh, so, how did I help you?"

"You chose the second one I caught. I told the first one that if she kept kicking up a fuss I'd give her to you, and you'd butcher her like a hog. After watching you take that other one, she's ready to do anything at all I ask her to just to stay out of your clutches."

"Yeah? You think that'll speed up the process, do you? I should charge you more rent."

"It's getting late, Albie, let's get this show on the road. I'll make mine watch you have your fun then start her training. This'll be good."

Still gloating and making their plans, they left the house and headed for the barn. They were halfway there when they heard the sound of the engines.

"What the hell is that noise?" asked Albert, looking all around fearfully.

"Motorcycles," gulped Merle, "way too fucking many motorcycles. The Angel's found us. Run, Albert."

He ran towards his car, but the motorcycles turned into the driveway and raced towards the house. The bike in the lead had a small rider with long blonde hair streaming out behind her. Merle turned and ran the other way.

The Hard Way Back

When he realized he couldn't make it, Merle turned and ran into the open field. It did him no good at all. The bike roared past him then spun around in the dusty farmyard. Merle was facing the Fallen Angel.

While Merle made his run, Albert ran back to the house to get his shotgun. He made it to the door when a motorcycle roared up the steps and crashed through the door after him. The female rider grabbed him by the collar then turned the bike and drove back outside, dragging him alongside. She threw him to the ground at the feet of another woman.

"Good job, Mai. Thanks. All right, Albert, hand it over."

"What? Hand over what? You people are trespassing. Get the hell off my land."

"That remote in your pocket, hand it over."

He didn't move but another of the gang did. "Oh for fuck sake," snarled a young woman's voice as she advanced on him. Before he could react she drove a vicious kick into his belly driving the air from his lungs. She kicked him hard again, in the balls. "Give her the remote. Give her the fucking remote or I'll kick you to death then take it off your battered corpse." She followed that with a savage kick to the ribs.

"All right, all right," he gasped, as he tried to crawl away. His hands shook as he pulled the remote from his pocket and tossed it towards Penny.

Ryder scooped it up. "Where, Blue?"

"Just inside the barn, Ryder." She nodded and headed for the barn. "I got this. You guys do what you do."

Ryder entered the huge barn through the big door. She didn't see anything familiar. With a shrug of her shoulders, she stepped inside and activated the remote. The floor suddenly moved beneath her feet and, with a yelp of surprise, she leaped aside.

The section of floor swung up and away exposing the stairs going down. She heard a soft whimper of fear as she started down. "Hey down there, are there any lights in here?"

"Help us, please help us."

"I will, just as soon as I find the damned lights ... ah, there we go." As the lights came on Ryder saw things she recognized, and hated. She was in a torture chamber again, but this time it was different.

"Over here, please hurry before he comes back."

"He's not coming back, girl. I just kicked the shit out of him, and now the Fallen Angel and Lady Blue have him, if he's not already dead. Just give me a minute to find something to bust these locks with."

"The keys are over there," said one girl, trying desperately to point through the wire of the cage.

Ryder looked where she was pointing and saw a ring of keys hanging on the walls. In short order she had both girls out of the cages and into her arms, crying. "It's okay, it's okay, Ryder's got you. Come on now, my sisters, let's get you back into your clothes and out of this shit hole. Come on now, I'll stand guard while you get dressed."

They hurried into their clothes and, clinging to Ryder, swiftly climbed the stairs. Once out of the dungeon Ryder smashed the remote then led the girls out into the sun. They were just in time to see Albert and Merle meet their fate.

By the time Ryder had the girls out of the barn, Merle had been herded back toward the group. "That's far enough, Merle." He stopped walking and, trembling in fear, turned to face her. She got off her bike and walked around him until she was standing in front of the gang with her back to them.

"People, this man is Merle Downy. This is the piece of shit that slaved me out a few years ago. Take a close look, Merle, recognize me?"

As she spoke she pushed up that faceless mask she'd been wearing. "Come on, say my name."

His mouth worked, but it was a while before a sound came out. "Kara, you're Kara Jenkins."

"I was Kara Jenkins, but you ruined her, Merle. She had to get a new name. Do you know what that name is?"

"The Fallen Angel."

"That's right, Merle. You put Kara Jenkins through hell, and now the Fallen Angel is going to return the favor."

Kara hadn't seen Grace easing her way forward, nor had the others. As Kara raised her hands, and Merle wept, begging for a mercy that would not come, Grace acted. "Run, Master Merle," she screamed as she threw herself against Kara.

It was too late for Kara to stop it. The flame that leaped from her hand didn't reach Merle. Instead it engulfed Grace. In that instant several things happened at once. Grace screamed in pain as the fire took her, Merle made a break for it, and a wail of protest was torn from Kara's lips. "Noooooooooo!"

It all seemed to be in slow motion to Penny as she watched Mai go after Merle. She was running him down, but using just enough speed to catch him. "That girl takes too many chances," she thought as she returned her gaze to Kara.

Kara sat on the ground beside Grace's badly burned body, sobbing her heart out. "Penny, quick, heal her."

"What?"

"She's still alive," sobbed Kara, "heal her. I know you can do it, you and Moragah."

"Oh no, girl, this one's yours to fix. You burned her, you heal her."

"I can't, you know I can't do that do that anymore. Come on, Penny, hurry up. Heal her."

"Nope, you do it. Stop screwing around and kick that damned demon out of your head, call Moragah back, and save this girl's life.

She's an innocent, Kara. You've never killed an innocent and she doesn't have to be the first. Get off your ass and send that thing packing."

"Kill her, kill her now," screamed the voice in Kara's mind. "You have the power; you don't have to let her talk to you like that. Kill her."

Suddenly Kara leaped to her feet, pure rage and hate burning in her eyes. "You're right, I don't have to do what anybody says, not even you. Get away from me, I need Moragah."

"You need me. I'm the one who gave you true power. I'm the one who made you what you are."

"The hell you are. Get away from me. Moragah, help me. Moragah!"

At her cry the goddess came, thrusting light, blinding light, ahead of Her. Wave after wave of loving healing energy swept through the whole gang as they felt the vast presence of Moragah arrive.

"Begone from my daughter's presence, demon of darkness. She has broken your hold on her, and she is mine once again. Begone!

"Kara, my beloved daughter, my soul sings at your call. Hold your hands over Grace now and together we will heal her injuries."

"Moragah, I didn't mean to hurt her. I ..."

"Be at peace, Kara, for it was many others who hurt her and caused her to interfere. The fault is not yours and there is no stain on your soul. Quickly now, hold your hands over her and channel my energy to her. We will heal her injury together."

The others sat on their bikes, stunned by what they had witnessed, what they were witnessing now. The girl's poor burned body began to heal, new flesh replaced what had been burned away, and soon she was lying quietly, sleeping. When it was done, Kara collapsed.

Penny was at her side in a heartbeat, scooping her into loving arms where she lay sobbing. Thunder laid his jacket over Grace's naked body, for the fire had burned away her clothes.

Ryder and the two girls stood quietly near the barn. They had emerged in time to watch the healing and had felt the presence of Moragah. Ryder shook off the spell first and urged them gently forward to join the gang.

As Kara lay quietly in Penny's arms, Mai returned with Merle. She threw him on the ground beside Albert who had tried to crawl away during the action. Thunder had put a stop to that escape.

"So, are you okay now, Kara?"

"Yeah, Mai, I think I am. I've got some work to do, but I'm all right now."

"What do we do with these guys?"

Before anyone could speak, Penny pulled out one of her guns and shot Albert. His eyes tried to roll back to see the neat hole in his skull as he fell sideways. Penny spun the gun in her hand and passed it to Kara, butt first. "Go ahead, sis, finish it."

"Don't want a gun for this fucker," said Kara, as she stood up.

Merle scrambled to his feet and ran. Kara stepped past Penny and sent a lance of flame after him. He screamed and screamed as the fire consumed him. Kara walked over to his charred corpse and looked down. "You've stolen and tortured your last child, you bastard. If anybody thinks I'll feel guilty about killing you, they're wrong. I won't."

She turned and walked back to the gang. "Are you sure you're all right?" asked Mai, as she stepped closer.

"I will be, Mai," replied Kara, as she gave Mai a gentle hug.

"Kara."

"Yeah?"

"Get your hands off my ass right now." Everybody laughed at that and, smiling, Mai stepped back. "You are feeling better."

"Getting there," grinned Kara. "Okay, family, let's get the hell out of here."

She mounted her bike and led the gang back onto the highway. While the gang returned to the campsite for another night, Kara and Thunder rode into town to make a stop at the bar.

The bartender looked up as they entered. Kara gave her the thumbs up sign then turned and left. Back outside she pulled out her phone and called.

"Arlo."

"Angel here. Job done. Here's where you find the death camp."

She gave him the address and he wrote it down. "I'll send the authorities, Angel. Next time you're in town, drop by."

"Careful what you wish for, Arlo." She broke the connection then threw the phone in the dumpster. "I've used that one too many times," she said, as she noticed Thunder's raised eyebrow.

"So, back to the campsite now."

"Yup, I'm beat and need a few days rest."

"Wanna pick up some beer on the way?"

"Sure, why not. That shit tastes like horse piss, but I've developed a taste for it." His great bellowing laugh brought a smile to her face as they rode away.

Once back in the campsite Kara sought out Penny. She sat beside her, but didn't speak. After a long silence, Penny leaned against her and gave her a nudge. A moment later Kara leaned over and nudged Penny who started to laugh as she nudged Kara back.

"Are we okay, Penny?"

"Better than, sweet sister, better than. I'm so thrilled to have you back. How does it feel?"

"Awesome. I can feel Her all around me, guarding me, nurturing me. That deep burning ache inside me is gone. That thing is gone, gone from inside me. I have to admit I'll miss the strength and power it gave me, but the price was way too high."

"That abomination gave you nothing, Kara my daughter. The sudden burst of rage you felt when you locked eyes with your former tormentor

unlocked the power within you. That strength and power were always there, you were just unwilling to release them in fear of what you might do.

"The demon lied. It saw the chance and took it, making you believe it was the source of your strength, but that was not so. All it could really do was take advantage of your vulnerable state to drive the wedge between us. It was able to maintain that only by lies and distraction. When your heart cried out for me I was able to break through.

"I've made a few small adjustments, Kara. That will never happen again, it cannot happen again. Rest assured; I will be more careful in future."

"Moragah, I'm so sorry ..."

"Hush now, Kara, my beloved priestess. All is well. Through all your hunting and vengeance you never once harmed an innocent. Even under the spell of the darkness, you brought no harm to an innocent. Even when it tried to force you to fight Penny, you defied it and would not harm a sister priestess.

"Kara, you are even stronger than I believed, stronger than the dark believed. All is well, my daughter. As you sleep this night I will restore your body, for the battles you fought this day have taxed you sorely."

"Thank you, Lady Moragah. I swear to you, I will never again use the full extent of my abilities unless it's in defense of the weak and there is no other option."

"Be at peace now, Kara. Welcome home."

Penny smiled and tossed a blanket over Kara as she settled down to sleep. She had her sister back and she was content. The rest of the gang settled down as soon as Marla and Ryder returned from taking the two rescued girls to the police station.

As Ryder stretched out she once again did something she rarely did. She prayed. "Moragah, I know you're real because I felt you today. I'm glad you got Kara back, and thank you for healing Grace. That poor girl is all messed up in the head. If there is anything you can do to help her, that would be great."

Ryder's eyes popped open as the goddess actually replied. *"It is already done, Ryder. Grace will be content to return with her uncle tomorrow and she will be happy at home. Have no fear for her. Ryder, is there anything I can do for you?"*

"Thank you, Lady Goddess, but I'm okay. I have a good life here with the Chosen. Take care of Angel. She'll need that for a while." Ryder felt the goddess's mirth as She pulled back and sent a wave of loving energy through her. While a bemused Ryder lay there mulling over the fact she'd just had a conversation with a goddess, Mai rolled over, and grinning, went to sleep.

The next day they dropped Grace off with her uncle. This time it was a tearful reunion. Kara waved as they drove away. "So, what now?" asked Penny. "We going hunting again?"

"Go home, Penny," sighed Kara. "Your woman must be frantic by now, that or she's found a new sugar momma."

"Hush you." Penny laughed and swatted at Kara who leaned out of reach. "You sure you'll be okay?"

"Yeah, I'm all good now, big sis. Go home to your woman."

"What about you?"

"Me? I'll ride with the Chosen for a while yet, and then I'll head home to see if I can patch things up with the family."

"Ken will be thrilled to see you back to your old self again, honey. You know that's true."

"Yeah, I know. Go on, get out of here." Penny gave Kara another hug then rode away, heading towards the airport.

Kara turned and Mai was there. "You too, pretty girl?"

"Yeah, me too. I have stuff to take care of, and I've been neglecting it."

"You could stay with us."

"Will you keep your hands off my ass?"

"I'll try," grinned Kara, "but I doubt I'll be able to resist."

"Oh, that's it, I'm outta here." Mai revved up her engine and started away. Suddenly she wheeled the bike around and came up beside Kara. She leaned over and gave her a kiss on the cheek. "Take care of yourself, sister Kara."

"You too, Mai. Don't take any chances."

"I won't," sang Mai, as she rode away heading for the highway north, back to Seattle.

"So, now what for us?" asked Ryder.

"These guys have been on the road for months, Ryder. Some of them actually have homes to go to. How about it, guys? We go home, catch a rest, tune up the bikes then see what life has to offer?"

"Sounds good, Angel," agreed Thunder. They rode away towards the highway. A week later they were back in the same garage where they had first met Kara. She hugged them all in turn and Ryder a second time, then rode away, heading east.

"You think she'll ever be back this way, Thunder?"

"Who knows, Ryder, who knows. So, did I see you one hand Kyle's bike onto the lift?"

"Ah-huh, it was easy."

"Right. Easy. Okay, there's the computer, internet is hooked up, start studying."

"Studying what?"

"Whatever you like, Ryder. Just try to learn something useful."

"Useful. Got it." She settled down at the computer. "I wonder if they have World of Warcraft on this thing."

⸺⬤⸺

THREE DAYS LATER KEN Jenkins heard a soft knock on his door. "Come on in, it's open." He heard the door open then close again. He put down the book he was reading and turned to see who his guest was. It was Kara, a contrite expression on her face and shuffling her feet.

"Hi Grandpa, mad at me?"

"Kara!" He was out of his chair and had her in his arms in a heartbeat. "Oh my god, Kara. No, sweetheart, I'm not mad at you. I never was. Worried about you, yes, but never angry with you. Did Penny catch up with you?"

"Yeah, she did," replied Kara, as she snuggled in his arms. "Big sister followed me around, nagging and tormenting, helping even, until she managed to get through to me."

"She truly does love you like a sister."

"Yes she does. Penny is awesome. Grandpa, I won't stay long, I know the cops are probably watching the place, probably have it bugged too. I just wanted to let you know Penny brought me back and everything is good now."

"I can't tell you how relieved I am, Kara. Have you been to see your mom?"

"Yeah, I just left her place."

"Can I ask you something?"

"Sure."

"If you're here, how is it possible the Fallen Angel killed two pedophiles in Seattle last night?"

"Danged if I know, Grandpa." Kara grinned and sent a silent thank you to Mai. That girl was still on the hunt and keeping the eyes of the authorities away from Kara for a while.

From her grandfather's place Kara returned to New York for a while then resumed her hunt for pedophiles, but this time it was for the sole purpose of freeing the victims and stopping the abusers forever.

More Musings

"What would have happened if Kara had gone over to the darkness completely? She would have killed both Mai and Penny, then hunted down any new priestess I might create. I would have needed to make a warrior well before I was ready, and while I was focused on defeating Kara, the dark would have been free to create any number of agents of evil like those pedophiles Kara has hunted down.

"Fortunately, Penny was able to challenge her at just the right moment, push her in the right direction. No, it was not I who sent Grace against the Angel to save the slaver, it was the dark demon.

"It believed it could use that to force Kara to kill Penny. Penny was able to turn that event against the darkness."

"Kara is fine now. I fixed the error I made in her, and I have made certain that none of the priestesses are in danger of the same fate."

The End

And now for a peek into book three in the Children of the Goddess series.

Lady Justice

by

Prudence MacLeod

Justice?

Tasha paced about her bedroom, fuming. Grounded? Sent to her room? She was twenty years old, for Christ's sake. She had taken part in a protest march, not a riot. She yanked the elastic from her long dark hair in frustration. Dammit anyway, this was wrong, so wrong. "I marched for justice, but there's no justice for me."

With a deep sigh she stepped before the mirror and took in her exotic looks. Her mom was first nations, and her dad was black. She had the long straight hair, high cheekbones, and lighter colouring of her mother plus the flashing eyes and dazzling smile of her father. That smile was nowhere to be seen this night.

Grounded, yeah, right. The hell she was. "I seriously need to get my own place." She swiftly dressed in black tights and tank top. A few essentials and spare undies in her backpack and she was ready to go. Tasha was just climbing out her window when she heard the front door crash inward. Loud shouts of "Get on the floor, Nigger. Now!" There were more shouts, her mother's scream, and then the gunfire.

Shocked, horrified, and trembling, she stood frozen, her stomach heaving, and listening to the voices from the main floor. "God damn it, Murdock, what the hell is wrong with you? Now we have to cover this up and hope like hell it doesn't cause another riot."

"He tried to kill me; you saw it Jim."

"I didn't see a damn thing, Murdock. He was unarmed and so was the woman. All right, boys, it's a goddam mess now. Search the rest of the house, find that damn kid and shoot to kill. No point making this any worse than it is. Damn niggers anyway. And make sure you get that cell phone."

At that command Tasha came back to life. All those years of gymnastics in school proved useful as she climbed out the window and swung up onto the roof. It was none too soon.

She heard the boots on her bedroom floor then the voice. "Ah crap, she was here, but she got out through the window. Probably three blocks away and crying to the media by now. There'll be hell to pay for this one. Shit. All right, let's get back to the station and get our story straight."

Trembling in fear, Tasha Stewart clung to the gently sloped roof, tears streaming down her face. It was over an hour later the ambulance and coroner arrived, but by then she had reached the ground and was gone. As the sun rose over the horizon, she broke down and sobbed her heart out in the basement of an abandoned building. "I didn't even go in to say good-bye to them," she wailed.

It took most of the day, but she cried herself out. Hunger eventually drove her out onto the streets. It wasn't until she tried to pay for the sub sandwich that she realized she didn't have any money with her, and she dared not use a bank card. She'd have to go back to the house.

Half a block away she spotted it, an unmarked police car. The house was being watched; they were looking for her. It suddenly hit Tasha that she'd been the original target all along. Her parents had been killed because of her. God damn it all, she'd only gone to a protest rally. They weren't terrorists.

They'd be called that, though. She burst into tears again and fled back to the abandoned building. She spent the night shivering in fear and the cold. She cried herself into a fitful sleep.

Tasha awakened slowly, fear gnawing at her very soul. She was no longer alone in the cold damp basement. The small hairs on the back of her neck were standing up and a shiver crawled slowly up her spine. "Relax woman," sighed a soft feminine voice. "I'm not going to hurt you." The speaker was a small girl not much older than Tasha. She had blue spirals painted on her face and arms.

"Who are you? What do you want?"

"I'm called Lady Blue. My name is Kara. Your name is Tasha and you're in deep shit. I'm here to bring you an option you might not have thought of. Hungry?"

"What do you mean options? Wait, what? Yes, I'm starving. Have you got anything to eat?"

"Sure, try this." She tossed Tasha a couple of military ration bars then fished a bottle of water out of her backpack. She passed it over.

Tasha forgot everything in her hunger. She devoured the bars then guzzled the water. A moment later she became aware of the small girl watching her. "These are military rations, where did you get them?"

"I took them off a soldier who tried to rape me. Feeling better now?"

"Yes, I am, Thanks. Wait, what did you mean about options? What were you talking about? What do you know about me?"

"I know all about you, Tasha. I know what happened to you and your family. I wish I could stay and help, but I have another errand that can't wait." She began wiping the blue greasepaint off her face. "Here, take this and wipe your face; you've got mascara everywhere from crying." Tasha gratefully accepted the offered wipe and cleaned her face.

"Better?" Tasha nodded her thanks. "Tasha, I know what you're thinking of doing. Bad idea, girl."

"Wait. What? How do you know what I'm thinking? Are you psychic or something? Can you read minds?"

Kara smiled at that. "Nope. I know because Moragah told me. She told me everything. Moragah knows you want to kill those guys and she wants to talk to you about that."

"Who or what is Moragah?"

"Moragah is the goddess of wisdom, defender of the weak."

"A goddess. Right." Tasha rolled her eyes then shrieked as Kara leaped to her side.

"Relax, woman. Geez. I'm not going to hurt you. Take my hand."

Reluctantly, Tasha reached out and took the small hand in her own delicate fingers. Instantly she was aware of that vast presence surrounding her, comforting her, driving the pain and anguish from her mind. "Do not fear me, my child. I will not harm you, but yes, I do exist." There was warmth and humour in that voice that sounded in her mind and Tasha relaxed completely. "Listen to Kara; hear what she has to say with an open mind."

At that, Kara released Tasha's hand and the presence of Moragah withdrew from her awareness. She shivered as the cold and dampness of the old basement returned. "All right, now that we have that out of the way..."

"Okay, that was totally weird...but nice. I don't even care how you did it. So, what's the deal?"

"The deal is simple. You want to kill those guys who shot your family. I don't blame you for that; I would too. However, that'll just get you killed as well. Moragah wants something more for you. She wants to help you, and She wants you to help Her."

"Ah-huh. So, what does this magic goddess of yours want to help me do?"

"What you want to do; what you wanted to do before this happened. She tried to prevent that, but I got here too late."

"Too late for what?"

"To stop what happened to your family. I was halfway across the country when I got the call. I'm sorry, Tasha."

"Stop it? How could you have stopped it?"

"I have my ways," sighed Kara. "It's all changed now. At first I was supposed to stop the killing of your family then talk to you about your efforts to bring justice to the people of this city; your crazy desire to help people even though they don't want anything to do with you because you're not like them. Now it's all changed. Something else has come up and I have to move on."

Kara rose to her feet and reached for her backpack, but Tasha stopped her. "Wait, that voice said to talk to you..."

With a sigh, Kara sank back to a cross-legged position on the floor. "Okay, here's my story. I was twelve when I was kidnapped in front of my school. I was raped and forced into prostitution out on the west coast. A few years of horror later I was rescued by Lady Blue."

"Lady Blue, you said you are Lady Blue."

"One of. I was made a priestess of Moragah after the rescue. I couldn't fit back into a normal life, you see. Anyway, we call ourselves Lady Blue. I have no real idea why, but I think it has something to do with the sacred spirals we paint on our faces when we go to war with the bad guys. Moragah made me a priestess; that gave me a reason to stay alive. Now I kick ass, take names, and stay one step ahead of both the cops and the criminals I fight."

"Kick ass, right."

"Hey, I may be small, but I'm mighty," grinned Kara.

"Ah-huh."

Kara sighed and lowered her eyes to the floor. "I see a demonstration is in order."

Tasha shrieked as Kara exploded from the floor and blurred out of sight. She was moving too fast for the eye to follow. A support post was yanked from its station and the floor groaned above them as the post was shattered into splinters. Kara came back into view, breathing deeply. She glared at the wood, and it burst into flame. A moment later Kara reached out her hand and closed it into a fist; the flames died instantly.

She smiled at Tasha who sat pressed tightly to the wall, her hands covering her mouth. "That's just a sample. I can do other things too. For example, I always know what direction to go, I can hear at distance if I concentrate. You know, stuff like that."

"Oh my god," Tasha breathed softly.

"A priestess of Moragah has superpowers, we all do. Some are different. For example, Penny can run right up the side of a building. Man, she's awesome."

"How many of you are there?"

"As far as I know there are three of us now. Look, I have to go. Talk to Moragah before you do anything else, okay? Just talk to Her. If this life isn't for you there'll be no hard feelings." Kara swept up her backpack and jogged up the stairs.

"Wait. What???"

"Talk to Her, Tasha, just talk to Her. Don't do anything else until you talk to Moragah." With that, Kara disappeared through the door.

Tasha ran up the stairs, calling for her to wait. "Hold on a minute..." She stood gazing all around, up and down the street. There was no sign of Kara, the tiny wonder woman. "How the hell did she...? Oh well, that was all totally weird. Maybe I imagined it all.

"Doesn't matter. I need to go home. I need some cash, a shower, some of my clothes, and...oh god, Mom and Dad..." Fighting back the emotions that threatened to consume her, Tasha headed for what had once been her home.

The house was still being watched. Dammit anyway. Tasha faded back along the street and pulled out her phone. It was dead. Double damn. She knew she couldn't continue on the way she had been. She needed help so she headed towards her best friend's place.

That house was being watched too. What the hell? She circled around to the alley behind the house and whistled softly. On her third try she got a response. "Shhh, Tasha, is that you? Run, girl. The cops are everywhere looking for your head. Run."

She ran. Tasha had been back at her hideout for about an hour when she heard someone approach. "Tasha, you here?" called a soft voice.

"Denise, is that you?"

"No, I'm somebody else. Of course it's me. Who the hell else would it be? Don't look so disappointed. Who were you expecting, Wonder Woman?"

"I had hopes," sighed Tasha as she sank to the floor and rested her head in her hands. "Man, I am so screwed."

"You'll be worse than that if they catch you, girl." Denise sank to the floor beside her. "What did you do?"

"Nothing, I swear, Dennie. I went to that protest rally, but it was pretty peaceful. The cops threw their weight around, but nobody started anything. As usual they denied shooting that guy, the politicians promised to get to the bottom of it, and nothing at all will ever come of it. Same shit, different day.

"It started to break up, so I went home. When I got there, Mom and Dad were in a fit. They tried to ground me, for god's sake. Oh god, Mom and Dad..." She burst into tears again and Denise put her arms around the distraught girl. "Sorry," sniffed Tasha as she regained control of her emotions.

Denise released her then sighed. "The cops say you were on drugs, went nuts, and shot both your parents."

"Sure I did. Did they explain how I managed to have a loaded police special?"

"No," chuckled her friend. "They left that part out. Look, Tash, you gotta get out of town. Things have gone completely crazy around here now. You know those guys will shoot you on sight. Tash, I don't think the Association will help you either, you know..."

"You mean because I'm not black; I'm just a mutt?"

"Hey, you know Mr. Gimbal didn't really mean that. He was just upset and..."

"Let his true feelings slip?"

Denise hung her head and sighed. "Yeah, maybe. It's just fear talk, Tash, you know that. Everybody is so damn scared for their lives these days. Shit, if my dad even thought I was here talking to you..."

"He'd freak, right? It's okay. He just wants to keep his family safe. I get that. Man, I am so screwed. I don't have any money, I don't dare use a bank or credit card, and I stink. I need a shower, I need clean clothes, and I need to think. You go on home, Dennie. Be careful and I'll let you know where I end up if I survive."

Denise kissed her friend's cheek, hugged her tightly, and then rose to go. "Here's twenty bucks. It's all I have."

"Thanks, sweetie. I'll pay you back...someday."

"You'd better. Be careful and get out of town as quick as you can. I won't see you again for a while, Tash. Dad is sending me out of state to college."

With that, her only friend was gone. Tasha sank into a depression and cried herself to sleep. She dreamed. In her dream Kara, a taller blonde, and an Asian girl, all wearing blue tattoos, came and sat with their backs to her, guarding her rest.

Suddenly feeling safe, Tasha relaxed into a deeper sleep and the dream faded. She awakened several hours later, hungry but feeling rested. Refreshed.

Tasha went to the far corner and relieved herself then returned to the pile of crushed cardboard she'd slept on. It was time to make a plan. She couldn't go on the way she was, she had to do something, anything. Maybe she should talk to a lawyer. It was as good a plan as any.

Don't miss out!

Visit the website below and you can sign up to receive emails whenever Prudence MacLeod publishes a new book. There's no charge and no obligation.

https://books2read.com/r/B-A-ZKBBB-TKETC

BOOKS 2 READ

Connecting independent readers to independent writers.

Also by Prudence MacLeod

Children of the Goddess
Lady Blue
Fallen Angel

Forgotten Worlds
Suvi
Echo of the Past
Survivors
Ship
Fleet
Unite
IGEN
T.E.N.

Nova series
Novan Witch
Assassin of Nova
Beyond Nova
Claimstake
Red Nova

Watch for more at https://www.prudencemacleod.com/.

Telling a story is like knitting a sweater. Start with a ball of possibilities, pull out one small thread and begin. With luck and patience you will create something quite wonderful.

About the Author

On a far off windswept island Jennifer Crandall sits with her dogs and cats creating fantastic stories for all to enjoy. She publishes as JL Crandall, Prudence MacLeod, and Jenni Leigh.

Read more at https://www.prudencemacleod.com/.